FALSE STARTS

FALSE STARTS

Terri McFerrin Smith

ALFRED A. KNOPF
New York   1988

Library of Congress Cataloging-in-Publication Data
Smith, Terri McFerrin.
False starts.
I. Title.
PS3569.M53834F35   1988   813'.54   88-45212
ISBN 0-394-56866-4

Manufactured in the United States of America
First Edition

To
my son

Now the parable is this: the seed is the word of God.

—Luke 8:11

PART I

Ian's Mother

Mara blinked, then stared. Dim. White. Hundreds of off-white holes in the surface overhead. Holes forming rows forming ranks. Acoustical tile. Silent. White. Ceiling joining wall joining white wall. White cinder block. Six blocks over, two blocks down. Window. Light along the lines of the venetian blind. Shadow moving in the light.

As Mara swam up out of her sleep, objects took shape in the colorless room. A lamp, a stool motionless on its casters, a steel cabinet. Gleaming jars of cotton balls and tongue depressors. Mara closed her eyes, wondering where she might be. Unable to imagine a place so silent and simple, she dozed again.

Inhaling, she smelled a kindly, antiseptic odor. A cool hand lay across Mara's forehead, another stirred in her limp hand. This time, Mara's eyes opened wider, following the wrist to the forearm to the shoulder. A white figure.

"Miss Johnson?"

Mara didn't answer, thinking, This is the woman who wheeled the machine, the steamy jar of pulp away.

"How do you feel?"

Mara's tongue lay thick and dry in her mouth. Shrugging, she felt a clean white sheet rustle against the pale contours of her body.

"Why don't you sit up?" The woman helped raise Mara's body to a sitting position. A waxed, white floor spun into view.

"You just sit there a minute. I'll get your clothes."

Mara's feet dangled inches from the dizzying floor. She gripped the edge of the narrow chrome table where she sat. Her knuckles had turned white, when the door to the room opened. Mara stared past the perfect white figure in the doorway, out into a hall. Putting one hand to her head, Mara asked, "What time is it?"

"Five."

Somehow Mara knew the white figure, a nurse, would go off shift soon, home to cook the evening meal for her family. She thanked the woman for her clothes, her familiar clothes. "I'll be just fine."

The nurse nodded and left the room. Mara lifted her white gown overhead. She shivered. As Mara stood, she began to bleed.

Ether

To this day, Mara does not know what purpose tonsils and adenoids serve. In 1956, tonsillectomies were a popular, moneymaking operation. Mara was two. Her mother worked for Hallmark Cards at the time; her father studied tax law. Usually, Mara stayed home, eating toast in chicken broth each time she had a sore throat.

She doesn't remember much about the operation. Her mother took a day off from work. She held Mara's hand as they went up in the hospital elevator. Mara can remember the floor pushing at her feet, the void in her knees. She remembers how high the bed was from the floor. And slipping into a nightgown and being rolled away to a room where the doctor was. She recognized his face, kindly and old. She tried to do what he asked her to do, count to ten.

Mara did not know her numbers that far. She said, "One. Two. Three . . ." and then, the smell was too sweet. The dark swallowed the number four.

The Kitchen Table

Mara's mother eats because her father drinks. Her father drinks because her mother is fat. They eat and drink and blame each other at the very kitchen table they ordered to match the counter top in 1961. That was the year they built their dream house, a split-level on a hilltop. The Johnsons were among the first families to move into the development. From the hilltop, they watched identical split-levels rise up out of the holes around them.

The Formica on the kitchen table and the counter top is white with scribbles of black. It has always looked as though each of the Johnson children learned cursive writing on its surface. The counter top is stained now and etched with knife marks.

For years, Mara's mother stood at the kitchen sink cleaning fruits and vegetables. Mara could never understand how her mother had grown so fat; fruit and vegetables are not fattening. A psychiatrist once suggested her weight problem could be a nostalgia for days she'd been expecting, an attempt to refill her belly with food.

Mara's mother loved sweet corn, fresh from the field. She taught Mara to recognize a good ear; pull back the husk and sink a fingernail into a kernel. If it squirts a milky liquid, that ear is good. And she'd make a meal of green beans flavored with smoked bacon. One summer, she ate so many tomatoes, she developed a rash around her wedding band. Rather than give up tomatoes, she parked the ring on the windowsill above the sink until the first frost.

The family could look forward to homegrown tomatoes every Fourth of July and sliced peaches for the ice cream Mr. Johnson cranked out in his ribbed knit undershirt. Their mother would take the Johnson children to the orchard and let them lug the finest, most dangerous peaches they could find back to her basket. The fuzz irritated their forearms. They said the fuzz felt like kissing Daddy in the morning. Other times, they picked strawberries. Mara's brothers and sister crawled into the strawberry beds before the dew had dried in the morning. As they picked, they ate so many they longed to lie down in the dark wet earth between the rows and sleep off their stomachaches.

At the grocery store, Mrs. Johnson thumped and sniffed melons. In summer, when Mr. Johnson wouldn't be home for supper, Mara's mother would fix huge spreads of fresh vege-tables. For dessert, they'd all eat slices of watermelon and spit the seeds at one another. They believed if they swallowed the seeds, their bellies would swell around the melons that grew inside.

Her cooking was Mrs. Johnson's way of loving. However, she hated to clean up the mess. And as soon as Mara and her sister were tall enough to stand on chairs at the kitchen sink, they began to do the dishes. The Johnson sisters fought over who would wash and who would dry. They hated the silverware, the pots and pans. Their mother went to bed right after dinner and listened to her daughters fight.

When Mr. Johnson was home, the children fought at the dinner table as if they were somehow on display and anxious that he notice them. Many nights, he wasn't there. Mrs. Johnson set a place for him at the table and kept food warming. When the children woke the next morning to find the plate untouched, they carried a knot around in their bellies all day. Sometimes, his late arrival would wake Mara. Sometimes, she could hear him eat. Sometimes, she heard the cupboard door open and the deep voice of his bottle.

The children never understood why their arguments at the dinner table became so vociferous. They couldn't understand why none of them, not even Mara's mother, could win an argument with Father. Most of the time, Mother wouldn't argue. What can you say to a man who insists that males have the capability to suckle their young? She saw, Mara thinks now, that he drank out of pressure. He was under pressure because he was ambitious. No one knew why he was ambitious, but he had bills to pay, house payments to make. The Johnsons lived in the dream house on the hill. He provided for them. How could Mrs. Johnson take issue with that?

As the Johnson children grew, they learned the fine art of kitchen table debate. Rule #1: Never cry, as Mother did. Rule #2: Be able to back up an assertion with a reason. Mr. Johnson played the devil's advocate and asked why, why, why, until Mara's reasons dissolved. Mara's mother learned to rise above the argument and begin clearing the table. She'd refuse to listen or pretend to refuse. Sometimes, she'd just laugh and her fat would shake. Sometimes, tears would collect in the corners of her eyes. Even when Mr. Johnson was home, Mara's mother went to bed early. The children would be stuck, a half hour or more, while Mr. Johnson finished his argument. And then, Mara and her sister had the dishes to wash.

Mara thought about this peculiar logic of fathers as she wiped around her mother's garage sale treasures. Toothpick holders, salt and pepper shakers, spoon rests had begun to accumulate on the counter top since Mara left home. She turned off the overhead light and turned on the swag lamp over the kitchen table. The cupboards, the ruffled curtains, the rows of medicine bottles on the sill receded into darkness.

Once the children left, Mara's father had moved his accounting practice home. He puttered around the house all day, waiting for Mara's mother. After a day at the office, she would come home and prepare potato soup. Mr. Johnson nibbled on soda crackers between drinks and thought aloud. Mrs. Johnson seemed to listen. By suppertime, her husband was no longer hungry. Mara's mother went to bed.

In the cleaned kitchen, Mara lit a cigarette. She smoked and studied the configurations of smoke in the light for a message. Under that interrogatory light, the prodigal daughter supposed she should listen to her elders. She made a fresh pot of coffee and invited her father to join her for a cup. He laid his work aside. They talked about the state of the world, their own backyard, Mara's ambitions. They discussed Mrs. Johnson's problem: her bargains, her housekeeping, her appetite. Mara began to feel the familiar acid edge of cigarette and coffee in her belly. Her own thought, critical of her mother, pleased and preoccupied her. She did not hear her father go on to explain how he needed her, Mara's mother.

"You know," Mara said, "I love this old table." She swept their stray ashes into her hand, then brushed her palms together over the ashtray. She felt her way up the dark stairs, to a bed in the guest room.

Mara heard a cupboard door open, ice rattle in a glass. And just in case his daughter was still awake, Mara's father muttered, "Gotta get some sleep, gotta get some sleep."

The Accountant's Daughter

"Abortion encourages irresponsible sex," Mara said several nights later during dinner preparations.

"*No!*" her father said, drunk. These Scotch-inspired arguments often proved to be his most lucid.

Mara sipped from her own drink, and said, "It's nothing more than a form of birth control."

"Just what is irresponsible sex?"

Mara thought for a moment. Her father was exacting about definitions. "It's hopping into bed with no thought about the consequences of your actions. Men," she muttered, "are particularly good at it."

Her father ignored this last remark. Mara seemed fond of sexual distinctions lately. "What consequences?"

"Children, of course."

"But Mara, human beings make love because it feels good. It's not strictly procreation." He winked at Mara's mother.

"You're right. It's recreational too. It's both. The problem is that men don't have to think about the consequences.

Women do. Nowadays, most men assume women have taken birth control measures. They don't even ask."

Mara's vehemence on the subject surprised her parents.

"But the pill, IUDs. Those *are* women's responsibilities."

"What about rubbers? Vasectomies?"

"That last is pretty extreme."

Again, Mara agreed. "They might at least have the civility to ask, remind the woman, at least attempt to share the responsibility."

There was a lull in the conversation. No one knew quite what to say. Mara's mother studied Mara's face.

"What do you want to do? Cut men off?"

"Well, I've found out the hard way. You shouldn't hop into bed with someone who isn't willing to commit himself."

"Cut us off."

"Not at all. I just stopped using birth control. I tell them that." Mara's father looked at his daughter's face. "It's amazing how often they change their minds. They put on their clothes and go home. *Not* using birth control is the best contraceptive."

"But, honey, it's fun."

"Might be more fun if I wasn't the one who had to worry about babies."

"You can't change that. Men can't help the fact they're men."

Mara went silent. She'd heard this last comment as "boys will be boys" too often. Her reasoning was convoluted, she knew. She could no longer explain it clearly to others.

"What's wrong with having children?" Mara had changed her tone. "Why do they all think children are a risk? Isn't it simply part of being human?"

"Yes, but it's an immense responsibility."

Mara, looking at the framed photographs of her brothers and sister across the top of the piano, couldn't believe he'd said this. It was her mother who had always managed to be there when any of them needed a parent. They had joked that Daddy was away, making a million dollars.

"Yes, it is that." Mara wanted to ask him if any of his children had been unwanted. She'd come along within ten months of the Johnsons' wedding. "But you know what abortion does, don't you? The girl comes up pregnant. The father decides the responsibility is too much for him. It's easy, in retrospect, to decide twenty minutes were unconsidered. He doesn't have to undergo the operation. It doesn't happen to his body. He doesn't even have to help her through it, if he doesn't have the stomach for it. It's as though it never happened. It's not a matter of life and death to him." Mara shut up, realizing she'd said too much.

"Mara," her father said, shaking his head, "why do you want to be so punitive?"

"It's not punishment. It's simply asking your partner if lovemaking has the same life and death consequence for him as it does for you."

While Mara's father considered for a moment, she continued, "No, I'm simply asking my lovers to be as fearlessly human as they can be. For love to be all it can be."

How Mara Came to Be

Mara went west with a girl friend, on a Greyhound. They spent New Year's Eve curled up with their pillows in the cramped seats, rereading their diaries for the year. Melodramatic accounts of men they'd snuck into their dorm room.

The bottle of fine German Liebfraumilch they'd stashed in a pack traveled through the dark Wyoming landscape with a laugh. A neon sign woke Mara in Buffalo, but her girl friend slept and Mara felt no desire to go running into a tavern an hour after midnight to have the bottle opened.

In Billings, a blind man tapped up to the pair and asked directions. He wore a fine old suit and blinked as the sun came up. He was looking for a men's room. Mara pointed out what she thought might be the right direction, then saw the wet spot, like a saddle, between his legs. The dark wind whipped and her concern for his thin, chapped thighs did not last long. She crossed the street to an all-night cafe. It was orange and vinyl. Mara and her girl friend ordered homemade cinnamon rolls. Over coffee, they noted the growing number of pickup trucks in traffic.

Butte rolled up under the bus at noon. The cafes there were closed for the holiday. Without even a bowl of soup to reassure themselves, they wondered if they'd made a mistake. The pair sat on the bus, peering through their window at a sign that read WAITING ROOM. Through the plate glass door beside the sign, they watched the thick, crossed ankles of old women, worrying that they might board the wrong bus. Mara had come west with no knowledge of her destination. These close, heavy buildings, the gray sky and the smoke, like breath, frozen in it.

Though they felt better coming around the mountain, Mara's girl friend had already decided to go home again. She didn't mention it. Together, they laughed at a billboard warning that one Montanan contracted VD every hour.

Missoula was hung over. The Garden City had a crisp, peculiar stillness. No welcome. The depot was as dingy as all the rest had been. Outside, the sky was clear. A car or two eased through the thin snow, leaving long black lines down Broadway.

Mara and her friend carried their luggage across the street. The Palace Hotel would rent them a room at $4 a night. A motionless man in the lobby raised one gray eyebrow over his dark glasses as the girls boarded the elevator. Their shower, single beds, and old chenille spreads seemed luxurious to them. Mara's friend went right to sleep. Mara pulled a sheet of the hotel's yellowed stationery out from under the Gideon's in their desk drawer. She wrote, "Dear Mom and Dad, just a note. We have arrived safely in the 1940s."

Mara lit her first cigarette. While the smoke curled into the bed lamp's light, she searched the desk drawer for an envelope. She didn't find one, and improvised by folding the paper in thirds and taping it closed.

Hands

He showed up one day while Mara was baby-sitting. In his
boots and jeans and mackinaw and beard. He introduced himself as a friend of the child's mother. Mara let him in. He
took off the jacket. The plaid flannel shirt underneath made
him look like any one of the outdoorsmen who cruised Missoula's streets in their Blazers and their jeeps. Like them, he
had a beer belly. When he opened his mouth to offer Mara
the fish, a visible breath emerged. He had no lips to speak of,
his teeth bent back into his mouth. But his hands held Mara's
attention.

Mara told him she didn't know how to clean the fish. His
hands were ruddy and rough, the fingernails ragged as though
he cut them with a pocketknife. He was a big man to begin
with, but his hands were disproportionately larger.

While Mara rummaged in a kitchen drawer for a filet knife,
he lay the fish on a cutting board. The baby rode Mara's hip
and blinked as the man showed how to make the incision
behind the front gill. The knife's fine blade eased along the

spine with a slight sawing motion. Mara studied the stainless shine of the knife, the slow movement of his blunt fingertips and his face as he worked.

He flipped one side of the fish back, exposing the ribs. His blunt fingers showed how Mara should make a second incision between the flesh and the skin. He showed how with a gentle motion that lifted the flesh away, just at the edge of the knife's fine blade, she'd have a filet. "There's nothing to it. You try."

Mara handed the baby to him and flipped the carcass over. The texture of the fish was slimy. The baby squirmed, looking for a soft curve on the hard planes of his body. Mara's progress along the spine was fair. She clipped a couple of vertebrae. He was unconcerned, he said she'd be able to chew those few. The baby had tucked its legs up to either side of its belly and nestled against the man's pectoral muscle. Mara flipped the filet back at the tail, but severed it with her second incision. She saw the man's eyes roll, but he said nothing. This made separating the skin from the flesh nearly impossible. Mara tried, but the finished filet had quarter-sized spots of speckled, silver skin attached to it. He seemed to think she could eat the skin too.

"But how do you cook it?"

"With a little oil. Dip it in milk and egg, a little cornmeal and flour."

Handing the baby back to Mara, the man wrapped the fish remains in newspaper and dropped them in the trash. The filets, he put in a bowl and ran tap water over them. He left. Mara heard his pickup pull out of the drive while she changed the baby's diaper. She looked out the picture window after him, but all Mara saw was the gray slush of afternoon.

. . .

The next time he came to see her, Mara told him the fish had been good, the odor intolerable. He laughed that she knew no better than to take the fish carcass outdoors within a day's time. She studied his hands. He asked for one of the weak, long cigarettes Mara was learning to smoke. They traded the stories of their lives. She was an accountant's daughter from a midwestern suburb. He was the third child of his father's third wife. He'd grown up in a little town on the Milk River.

Working Men

From the moment Mara entered the Hideaway Club, she felt she'd been there before. She was sure she'd dreamt about this garage turned bar in the months before she'd come to the last wilderness on earth. She watched the waitress's wet rag leave swipe marks on the chrome table. The guys were on a first-name basis with "Katie," a woman Mara guessed to be about fifty. Her hair stuck together with hair spray. She wore costume jewelry and a conservative polyester slack suit. She took no guff from the working men she served.

Mara listened to the guys talk of Alaska, the pipeline, the inflated wages and prices. If they could find a way to beat the cost of living, they thought they could make their fortunes, enough to get ahead, in six months' time.

"Hey, Mara, you could strap a mattress to your back and come along." Lane, the taxidermist, and Rick, Mac's partner, laughed. Mara smiled, not getting the joke and looked to Mac for direction. Tipped back in his chair, Mac's eyes smiled, but he didn't grin.

Mara said, "Oh, you guys."

Mac ordered another round of beers. Mara had so many lined up in front of her, she asked Katie not to open any more. "Bring me a tomato juice." Diluting her beer with juice, Mara could keep up with the guys.

"Couldn't Skip put us up?"

Mac nodded tentatively. Mara stood and crossed the linoleum floor to a pinball machine that flashed curvaceous women. She plugged a quarter in and stood back at arm's length with her middle fingers on the flipper controls. Her bottom wiggled with each thrust of the flippers. She was just learning to play pinball. It was a pastime she'd picked up with Mac. She didn't want to think about him leaving and she didn't feel right saying "don't go." She comforted herself with the thought that they only had a place to stay. Skip was a government bush pilot, no one with connections on the pipeline. They wouldn't go.

Mara lost her quarter to the machine and went back to the table for another coin. Rick's laugh filled the echoing emptiness of the bar. The laugh was so crazed and long, Mara wondered if he wasn't high on something besides alcohol. The laugh was so contagious, she smiled herself as she joined the circle again. She knew little about Rick. He'd had two wives, two children by the first. He was bogged down with child support payments, some $2,000 behind. Last year, unable to make sense of all his work-related receipts, he'd decided not to file an income tax return. Now, a little man from the IRS appeared at his door. The little man confiscated a rifle here, a stereo there, in lieu of delinquent payments. The little man threatened to throw Rick in jail if he didn't pay.

The joke was about a credit card. Rick would pay his delinquent taxes with a credit card! He fell off his chair laughing.

On all fours, he crawled under the table and bit Mara on the leg. She slapped him away and he sighed, as if to say, what do women want? As he stood, every contradiction about him stood out. This farmer's son from North Dakota styled his hair. His face, unlike Lane's and Mac's, was clean-shaven, yet he wore their same flannel shirts. Mara found him attractive and looked away.

Lane's laughter subsided first and he stared into his beer. "I wish I could go, but I'm months behind at the shop."

The shop, a taxidermy studio, was a hodgepodge of skins, racks, and wild game forms. Entering it for the first time, Mara felt herself in the northwest. She had not known the difference between an elk and an antelope, a sheep and a goat. Taxidermy was Lane's compromise between art school and the real world. Once he put wheels on toilets and skis on bicycle frames; now his reputation for lifelike, inexpensive mounts extended the length of the Bitterroot Valley.

Mara thought he'd be caught up if he wouldn't spend so much time trading tall tales with every hunter who came into the shop.

After three beers, he asked, "Wanna pose for me, Mara?" She met his hazel eyes and managed a playful no. Lane was married to a second wife. The wife was a friend of Mara's, but Mara wouldn't have taken her clothes off for any photographer, even an amateur.

She studied him as he looked into his beer with pretended dejection. He'd never have a beer belly. His own hips were slender and girlish. His hair was long, thick, and dark as his wife's. The grime under his fingernails contradicted his wrists. His face, at thirty, was lined from working with a taxidermist's chemicals every day.

Conversation slowed as happy hour ended. Mara could tell

each man was seriously thinking of Alaska. Lane looked up with a beer froth caught in his sparse mustache. "No, Linda would never understand even a hunting trip to Alaska." Rick and Mac nodded their understanding. Mara said nothing. Drinking, though she was learning to do it, bored her. She looked away from their sad faces. Katie flirted with an older man at the bar and laughed a seductive, throaty laugh. Cigarette smoke curled into the air.

Mara took fifty cents from the change piled for Katie's tip in the center of the table and slipped it into the jukebox. She made seven selections. Linda Ronstadt's "Prisoner in Disguise" began to waft through the air. The boys were putting on their jackets to leave.

Hunting

Early one autumn morning, Lane, Rick, and Mac took Mara hunting. At the hour Mac shook her awake, it was so dark Mara doubted whether she could distinguish a deer from the side of a barn. Even the trees swam together in one darkness. But she'd talked about this so long, target practiced all summer, purchased all the credentials, that she didn't roll over and go back to sleep.

Mac stood over her in a red and black checked jacket as she slipped thermal underwear over her sleep-warm body. He was impatient as she misbuttoned her flannel shirt. He laced up her boots as she braided her hair. And finally, he propped her up in the pickup as he scraped windows, revved the motor, and wound his quiet way downtown.

"You remember the rifle?"

Mac didn't answer, just parked out front of the Stockman Cafe and waved. Lane and Rick motioned from a table inside. Steam rose from their coffee cups into the bright overhead light of the cafe. Rick's fluorescent orange jacket seemed so bright to Mara she wearily closed her eyes. When she opened them again, Lane scratched one skinny leg inside his wool trousers. The conversation began without her. A cheery waitress brought her coffee and stood waiting for their orders. Mara gathered a big, greasy breakfast must be a ritual of the big hunt, but she was not a breakfast eater and waved the waitress away.

Mac, Rick, and Lane discussed places they might hunt. They wanted a place close to town, with mild terrain, since Mara was along. A place where they wouldn't have to contend with other amateurs, out-of-staters. Sopping up the egg yolk on their plates with triangles of toast, they chose a spot up the Blackfoot River.

The place, thirty minutes outside of town, surprised Mara. Dimly she recognized the rickety railroad bridge. Could there have been deer present that hot August afternoon Mac stood around her, pulling the rifle into her shoulder? She'd laid her cheek against the stock, finger on the trigger, anticipating the dust ghosts she'd raise.

A gate barred the old logging road. Lane and Mac, with ammo belts slung under their bellies, stepped deftly around it and began to climb the hill. Mara slipped the Smith & Wesson .22-250 from its case and ran her hand along the blond wood of its stock. She loved this gun. It was lightweight, and according to Mac, it was versatile. You could use it on all sizes of game. Its recoil did not leave a hickeylike bruise on Mara's shoulder like some of his other guns did. And the wood grain was beautiful, enough to want to polish it with lemon oil. Mara filled her pockets with shells and set off beside Rick. She could no longer see Lane and Mac up ahead.

Mac had told her Rick was not much of a hunter. Judging from the stories, it seemed the only deer he'd ever brought down he'd hit as it jumped out of the path of his car. True to what she'd heard, he hung back, wanting to talk in hushed tones.

Two figures appeared in the path up ahead, waving a red bandanna. Rick laughed and Mara turned to see what this meant. "Putting out a little wolf bait," he muttered. And Mara understood they'd squatted behind a tree and left their own human droppings.

At the crest of the hill, all four stood together, surveying the ridges and the valley, deciding on a plan of attack. Rick and Lane would circle to the left, Mac and Mara to the right. Then, at a spot Mara couldn't identify, they'd meet and flush back down the mountain.

Mara set out beside Mac. Within seconds, he whispered at her, "Walk flat-footed, it will cut the sound you make." Mara grew so absorbed in stepping without breaking a twig that she was unaware how far ahead of her Mac was. She heard a sound and looked up, around the rifle barrel pivoting with her shoulder. Mac stood tapping a can of snoose and lifting a plug of tobacco to his mouth. He waited for her to catch up.

"This here is a bed, a good sign," he said, pointing to Mara's feet. She stepped back and saw a flat, circular spot about the size of a curled-up dog. A spot covered with pine needles. She squatted and touched it, unable to feel any warmth. "You'll wanna look for fresh droppings too, since there isn't any snow. No tracks."

Mara nodded as if she understood. Mac set off again. The ridge they walked seemed to climb interminably. Mara fell behind, though walking flat-footed came more naturally to her now. From time to time, she saw Mac pause up ahead and peer around the valley through a pair of binoculars. Apparently he saw nothing. He kept walking, shouldering matter-of-factly through the trees. The butt of the Smith & Wesson grew heavy in Mara's palm.

Mara figured they'd been walking a couple of hours now. Her mind began to wander: northwestern November was not much different from midwestern November, cold and bleak. She wondered about the deer beds, the does and their fawns. Once a year, in rut, the bucks butted heads for the privilege of certain does. The rest of the year, as far as Mara knew, the does fended for themselves. Mara tried to imagine fending for herself in the woods. She thought about Mac's rule that she could shoot only a buck, when a shot rang out.

She stopped. Ahead, Mara saw Mac freeze too in a half-crouch. Slowly, like an animal, she saw him ease to a stand from this position and look around, alert as she imagined a deer itself would be. Mara followed the direction of his eyes and perhaps a quarter mile away, she saw a spot of flickering orange move from tree to tree. It stopped. Rick's high crazy laugh echoed through the little valley.

Mara and Mac met Lane, each having completed the half-circle of the ridge. Mara was surprised to learn it was only eleven o'clock. She staggered, stubbing her toes against the inside of her boot. After the second time Lane and Mac paused to wait for her, Lane handed Mara the sling from his rifle. Wordlessly, she accepted it; she'd watched the empty barrel of her rifle swing back and forth at her waist, recklessly. The three headed downhill, Mac and Lane at a brisk pace, as if they were trying to tell her something. Mara's legs faltered with the attempt to keep up. She was hungry.

Mara kept the men in sight. Without them, she would have had no bearings, beyond going downhill. Curiously, she no-

ticed the conversation between them grew less hushed. They
paid less attention to the sound they made passing through
the brush. Then suddenly, they stepped out on the road. Mara
hadn't realized the road was this close. The hunt must be over
and she hadn't seen a thing. This, wandering around in the
woods, is hunting?

Mara brushed wisps from her braids away from her face.
She sniffled and heard the short, rhythmic shots of a .22. As
they came in sight of the truck, Mara could see Rick on the
tailgate, drinking a beer. He'd been far enough ahead to set
up some twenty cans on the opposite side of the river. Between
swigs, he took successful potshots at the cans. Mara heard their
slight metallic sound tumble down the rocky bank into the
river.

Mac and Lane said nothing as they slipped their guns back
into their quilted cases.

To Mara, Rick said, "You wanna try?" She looked at
the other two hunters. Unable to read their expressions, she
shrugged and said, "Sure." Taking the .22 from Rick, she
sighted according to the small metal piece jutting from
the far end of the barrel. The gun felt like a toy. It barely
kicked as it brought down a rusty can of Rainier on the first
try.

In the Beginning

In the beginning, they slept. Together, in a tropical room, a greenhouse, a sun porch walled in with windows. Plants drooped over the rims of their clay pots and grew toward the floor. Vines climbed the oak grain of the dresser and clung to the mirror. Fronds of fern stirred the air. African violets bloomed. Someone had tied back the blades of the sansevieria and spilled potting soil on the floor.

An edge of light crossed their faces. The girl blinked. In the night, their breath condensed on the windows. A drop of moisture rolled toward the sill. A planter revolved overhead. A chill touched her shoulder. The girl turned toward the boy. Her fingers caught in his auburn hair. She liked the warm, damp smell of their sleep. She closed her eyes.

In the dream, the sky and the earth were the same color. White. There was no horizon, yet there was a town built of alphabet blocks. Smoke puffed out of chimneys. Trees without leaves surrounded the houses. The trees took on human postures. Fat robins hopped from limb to limb. People made motions in their sleep, within the houses. The men went to work. The women drank coffee and said, "I'm going to have a baby." The sun, a visitor, strolled the streets, filling the trees with a violent red.

He woke. The walls were green, the windows dirty. A bare light bulb hung overhead. Dust mice skittered under the bed.

The Dishes

Each of them was the other woman in his life. There were exclamations, "I've heard so much about you." And hugs, as though each really did welcome the other. Then, "I held her at arm's length." A cold sore on the girl's lip, an odor of cigarette smoke about her. She noticed how tightly the mother's hair was wound around her green curlers; it was a red more faded than the girl's own auburn-haired mother.

The son grinned and tickled the mother. The same grin—silly, apologetic, and grim—spread across her face. Her wrinkles were filled with fat and the girl thought the mother looked younger than her fifty-five years. The mother slapped at her son's hands; the hands were the girl's favorite part of the man.

"You kids hungry? Want something to eat?"

The older woman peered into her refrigerator. The girl saw it was filled with forgotten leftovers. Jars with no pickles, moldy cheeses, small packages of crumpled aluminum foil.

"I've got meatloaf." The girl shook her head, but the son bent over the mother. The mother's housedress lifted, exposing deep dimples in the back of either knee. The son lifted out a gallon jug of milk and sat at the spot the girl cleared for him at the kitchen table.

The table was cluttered with newspapers folded to the crossword, bills and junk mail, a fat Bible in a zippered vinyl cover. He swigged directly from the bottle as the girl searched the clutter for an ashtray. He sucked the white liquid from his mustache and the mother sliced the gray, greasy meat.

In the months the girl and the son had lived together, the girl had never carried milk home from the grocery store. She didn't drink it herself. He'd never mentioned his own thirst for it. Neither did she know his favorite sandwich was meatloaf, drenched with ketchup.

Beads formed on the milk bottle at room temperature. His fingers drummed on the table. The girl gave up her search for an ashtray. She was very tired. Together, they'd driven slick roads all day, his truck full of her shifting belongings. The visual thump of power poles subsided east of Chinook, where the shutters of an abandoned church began to bang in the wind. It had grown dark and the nearer they came to their destination, the quieter Mac and Mara had become. He'd searched the dial for a radio station they both liked. She studied the dark prairie for darker forms that simply weren't there. They'd exchanged a look when the small collection of lights appeared on the horizon. His hometown.

She closed her eyes. She wanted to sleep. She heard the plate set down, a chair sigh with the mother's weight. A sandwich and a pickle. Mara lit a cigarette. Now the mother searched among the clutter for an ashtray. Unable to find it, she shuffled across the linoleum in her overrun slippers. She rummaged through a drawer of kitchen gadgets.

Mara's smoke curled toward the overhead light. She hated

overhead lighting, particularly at this hour of the night. It threw everything into too sharp a relief. Even skin took on a dull gray color. Just as the ash was about to fall from her cigarette, the mother set the lid of a jar down before Mara and sat again herself.

"You here to stay?"

The son nodded, his cheek full of meatloaf. The mother adjusted her bifocals on her nose and seemed to search for a word in the crossword. She erased something with the stub of her pencil.

"Well, until you two find a place, Mara can sleep on Nanna's old bed. There's a piece of plywood under the mattress, but it'll have to do."

Mara exhaled and lay the cigarette in the jar lid. She put a hand to the small of her back and rubbed as if to indicate a problem there. Tar collected in the lid and the mother continued.

"I made up the bed in your old room. You can sleep in there."

Mac finished the sandwich and wiped his mouth.

"It's full of your brother's schoolbooks and my plants, but it'll have to do."

The man nodded and rose, shouldering his way out the back door. Mara stubbed her cigarette out and listened to the clock tick. As if the mother had heard it too, she stood up and offered to show Mara the bathroom and her bed.

Mara sat on the edge of Nanna's narrow bed, studying the furniture in the room. She could hear mother and son murmuring in the kitchen, the sleeping breath of Mac's teenage sisters in another bed across the room. Eventually, he brought her suitcase and gave Mara a quick peck on the cheek. Out loud, Mara wished she had a nightgown.

He laughed as he walked on into the next room. He left his door slightly open and Mara undressed by the block of light it let into her room. Huge, leafy shadows played on the walls. She could hear him move heavy clay pots, pushing boxes across the floor, clearing a path to his bed. She heard the change loosen in his pockets as he removed his jeans. She heard his boots fall to the floor. She heard the lamp click off. She heard him punch his pillow and his restlessness subside, long before the dark entered Mara's head.

Mara slept late and soundly in Nanna's old bed. One morning as Mac left for work, she pulled his ear to her lips and whispered, "How will we make love?" The kitchen light flashed in his eye, but he shrugged his shoulders and turned to go. His back was covered with red and black checks.

Mara, barefoot and robed, sat down at the kitchen table, to her coffee and her cigarette and the Billings *Gazette*. She wondered how a paper from a town two hundred miles away arrived in time for breakfast. Beginning with the horoscopes, she read her way forward to the editorial page.

His mother bustled behind Mara, piling breakfast dishes in the sink.

"I'll do those, why don't you sit down?"

In this way, Mara had learned the history of her bed, the house, the town, and the mother herself. The bed, like the rocker in the living room, had belonged to Grandma Winters. The grandmother had lived with them in the early days of their marriage. Forrest's mother.

She paused and Mara nodded. She did not know what to

say. The picture the mother pointed out in the photograph album was of a cantankerous-looking woman in a polka-dot dress. Her hair in the black and white glossy was a steel gray of tight curls.

Mac's mother had removed her green curlers. She hadn't yet brushed the curls out and her head was covered with tunnels of hair. She ran her hand through the curls.

"Yeah, Forrest's mother had back troubles. She sat in that rocker all day and complained." Mac's mother grew lost in her thought. The dog scratched at the door.

"She was full of advice too. She had the years on me, but I knew enough. Seemed like I couldn't do anything right, plant cabbage or wash dishes. Well, that first year, the black-birds may have made off with the corn seed, but we had fifty head come up."

The woman continued as if talking to herself. "Once, after supper, Forrest put on his coat before he dried the dishes. We used to do them together and go for a walk afterwards. I asked him where in the hell he thought he was going and he said, 'Out.' I slammed the dishes around, then she called from the living room, 'How long did you think the honeymoon would last, honey?' I could feel her smile. She just rocked and rocked.

"She died fifteen years ago, just after we bought the house. Never got around to taking the board out of the bed."

Mara rose to fill her coffee cup. She put the morning paper on a pile of old papers in the pantry. Later, the mother would dig the crossword out of the pile on her way to work.

A tenant knocked on the door and shuffled into the room before the landlady could answer. Mara flew to her room to dress, going so fast past the rocker, it rocked once or twice.

Over the sound of water running in the bathroom sink, Mara heard a high old voice say, "Alice, you're gonna have to do something about that plumbing."

Mara could not hear the reply over the toothbrush in her mouth. She took a last pleased look at herself in the mirror and ventured back out into the kitchen.

Before an introduction could be made, the tenant said, "You must be Mara." The girl nodded at the fine wrinkled face of an old Indian woman.

"Well, you better not go flushing the toilet, my sink's backed up upstairs."

Mara did not know what to say. The woman slapped her thigh and looked out of her wrinkles with a keen animal eye. Her other hand bent around a mug of coffee, as if she lived at this kitchen table.

"Don't mind Louise, Mara." Mother Alice sighed. "The house is old. I'll call the plumber today."

"How old?"

"Well, I been here ever since they divided the upstairs into rooms. I came with the place." Louise cackled again.

Alice took her hand from under her chin and extended her arm. "This whole first floor used to be big enough to hold dances."

Mara could not imagine society of any sort in this dusty, cowboy town.

"There was a veranda clear around the front of the house. Big trees and lilac bushes in the yard." Mara could hear Alice imagine the luxury. "A maid lived in my room."

"Yeah, and you ought to see the stained-glass window in the stairwell up on the third floor."

"Three floors?"

Louise nodded. "Yep, four apartments upstairs and one in

the basement." She was visibly proud of her small place in the huge house.

"Any vacancies?"

The mother-landlady shook her head, no. "Forrest thought when he bought this place, it would be a moneymaker for us. He had big plans to renovate it, but the kids kept coming. There was never enough money. Gradually, he enclosed the porch for the kids."

Mara emptied the percolator and started a fresh pot of coffee. She preferred drip coffee.

"That room of Mac's?" Mara nodded. "It was so nice. Forrest walled it up with window 'cause it faced the east. So sunny in the mornings. I never had to wake the boys."

It sounded nice to Mara too. She tried to imagine the light inching across Mac's face in the morning now. He slept in the boys' double bed all by himself.

Louise, tiring of history she'd heard too many times before, put a veined hand on the table and pushed to a stand. Cryptically, she said, "I had to rub Limburger cheese on my nipples to wean that boy of mine. You call that plumber right away, Alice, you hear?"

The floor mat balled up behind as Louise closed the door.

Alice sighed and the coffeepot gurgled.

"Since Forrest died ten years ago, the house hasn't been anything but trouble. You think I could get Mac to regrout the tile in the bathroom?"

Mara shrugged. In the week they'd been in his hometown, Mac had spent his hours at home, lying on the couch, animated only by a Lee Marvin movie. A rerun of his father, forever hunting and fishing and walking to the telegraph office with a lunch pail banging against his knee. While Mara wrote letters in the easy chair, he received this message: OFFER HER MORE

THAN A TUMBLEDOWN HOUSE. STOP. "I'm seeing a side of Mac," she wrote, "I've never seen before."

"Eventually," Mara answered Alice.

"He installed the carpeting for me. Didn't he do a good job?"

Mara looked at the floor.

Mara began running water in the kitchen sink. This sinkful would take an hour. With the coming and going of Mac and the two teenage sisters, all cooking for themselves, the chore was never done. And Mara had never realized how particular she was about kitchens.

Over her shoulder, Mara asked Alice, "Know of any job openings in town?"

"Hospital. They're always looking for nurses' aides. Change bedpans and such."

Mara said nothing. The suggestion, she realized, was a serious one. Alice worked nights as a practical nurse. It was there Alice did her crosswords and knitted afghans so each of her children had a new one, once a year. There she delivered babies in the middle of the night, so as not to disturb the doctor's sleep. There she taught these newfangled mothers how to nurse, grabbing their breasts, putting the nipples in the babes' sucking mouths. Medical gossip peppered these morning conversations. Already, Mara felt she knew this little town too well.

"Anything else?"

"Well, you might check with the Nelsons. Ivan. He's a big wheel around town. Just opened a new bar. He'll be looking for waitresses and barmaids."

"Hmmm." Mara scrubbed at yolk stuck to a fork. She liked

this idea better. In a town this size there couldn't be many choices no matter what skills a girl had. Mara had some experience—wiping tables, tilting a glass under a tap just right. She reasoned, as she washed, it'd be a good way to meet people.

"I'll check it out."

By the time she said it, Alice had gone to bed for the day.

The Rocker

Grandma's rocker was a slender mahogany chair. For its age, Mara thought it had surprisingly simple lines. It had no arms. If a big person should sit in it, the chair would groan and disappear.

Alice kept it in one corner of the living room, the "ballroom" of Forrest's boardinghouse. Alice's clutter did not affect the dignity of the chair. The rumpled afghans on the overstuffed furniture, the newspapers, the dry dirty plates on TV trays kept a respectful distance. Mara noticed none of the family ever sat in the rocker or seemed to notice it was there, though as they flew in or out of the house, a current of air occasionally set it in motion.

Mara liked the way the chair looked, the way it would one day match her own antique chiffonier.

Several years later, Alice sold the boardinghouse. She moved into a spacious double-wide trailer. Mara went to visit. The trailer was considerably smaller than the house had been and the family, laughing, told how many trips to the dump it had taken to fit Alice into her new home. And still there was clutter.

The trailer came with its own furnishings and the worn overstuffed chenille sofa and chairs from the old house had been replaced by pieces upholstered in floral velveteen. When the sateen drapes at the windows were pulled, sheers fluttered into the diminished room. A black kitten stalked in and among the houseplants. The rocker moved with a breeze off the prairie.

Mara had acquired her own rocker at an estate sale. It had none of Grandma Winters' rocker's lines, but it had a dark finish that went well with Mara's antique chiffonier. There were no other bids on it. Mara thought she had a bargain at $50. She took the rocker home to her apartment and never bothered to sit in it. At night, on her blind way to the bathroom, she often stubbed her toe on one of its rockers.

The rocker sat in one corner of Mara's bedroom. It collected her clothes at night. Until the baby arrived, she didn't discover how indispensable rockers could be. She learned all of its creaks, and the creaks comforted Mara and the colicky baby. In the fifth hour of the first long crying spell, after she'd murmured, "We're separate now, we're separate now," Mara finally began to cry herself.

In time, the rocker, set to see the sun go down and the moon rise over the mountain, with its familiar creak and motion, came to be the most peaceful place in the world.

.   .   .

After six months of rocking, a crack across the seat began to widen and expose the fibrous wood under its dark stain. Mara had found the crack just minutes after the estate sale ended. Daily, she had polished the chair with dark oil, but its comforting creak turned to a moan. One day, the seat split clear across.

Still, Mara and the baby rocked in the anonymous rocker. Though it moaned and the crack pinched Mara's bottom, they nursed. And nursed. It was in such a reverie that the dowels connecting the chair's legs gave way. The seat yawned wide enough to deposit mother and child on the floor.

Mara put the chair in the Dipsty Dumpster.

Winter's Wheat

Mac's uncle's lips were as flat and reticent as the horizon where the wheat grew just south of the Milk River Reservoir. Behind his lips, his tongue was knotted, left that way by a grand mal seizure brought on, the doctors thought, by beer. It might have been the seizure that caused him to forget Mary Lou was adopted. Mac had not forgotten.

Tuff grinned and spat and gave Mara his daughter's vacated room when she and Mac showed up for harvest. Mac could have a bunk out there with the cats, he was going to bed.

As Mac moved a litter of kittens from his mattress to a cardboard box on the floor, Mara read the title of each Harlequin shelved in the headboard. She turned out the light to undress, listening to the brushing of teeth and the laboring toilet in the bathroom off her room. She heard sighs and, at long last, Tuff's snores from the hide-a-bed in the living room. As she drifted off to sleep, Mara realized she was being treated like a princess for reasons she did not yet understand.

Mara woke to sheer ruffled curtains and shades pulled against the flat, treeless horizon, long after the cousins had stood around in the shed badmouthing that no-good accountant husband of Mary Lou's who could help harvest only on weekends. "He'll probably end up with the place," Mac said, as Tuff checked moisture content and pounded his eccentric machinery with a wrench. Mara slipped into yesterday's jeans and stumbled into the kitchen.

Mac's aunt Sammy sat on her hemorrhoid pillow, watching sand cherries steam through the smoke of her cigarette. The fingers on her left hand spread as she sucked and gripped the cylinder again. "Coffee!" she announced, jumping up from her pillow. Sammy added a scoop of fresh grounds to the old, and more water.

The decor in the kitchen must once have been yellow and gray, Mara decided as Sammy asked, "How long can you stay?"

Mara sipped at her cup of hot brown water. "Two, three days."

"Mind if we just visit this morning?" Without waiting for a reply, Sammy asked, "You two gonna get married?"

"We haven't talked about it."

Sammy sighed, Mara unable to detect her relief. "Mac's a favorite of Tuff's, but he fell in love with Mary Lou when she was four. He rescued us. He looks like a grizzly character, but he rescued us. Brought us here."

"How long ago was that?"

"Good twenty-five years. Alice, all her brothers, married and moved away."

" 's good," Mara said of Sammy's cinnamon roll.

"I'll give you the recipe. I've had lots of time to practice over the years." Sammy gazed toward the kitchen window. Beyond it Mara saw high blue sky, yet the kitchen light was on as if Sammy could no longer see through the window.

Sammy began to lay out recipes for Mara to copy, sausage from the antelope Mac had not yet killed, the monster cookies she baked every harvest. Mara copied dutifully, as Sammy strained the cherries and added sugar.

"Yep, they moved away. Send the boys every year for their share of the harvest. Eat us out of house and home." Sammy stood at the stove, stirring constantly.

"Is there anything I can do?" Mara asked as Sammy poured the boiling liquid into jars.

"Just listen."

Mara heard chickens and dogs, a kettle of hot water rattle to a boil.

"We'll have us some hotcakes for lunch. Sand cherry syrup. Ever had sand cherry syrup?"

Mara shook her head as Sammy continued, "That's all that grows tall out there. You could take that laundry and hang it. Go have a look. I'll just be a minute."

The blue jeans hung heavy against the horizon. Mara scanned the yard for signs of activity. Nothing but Mac's dog cruising the cherry groves. Quonset huts, squat silos, tattered gray shingles on the house. The dusty evidence of a vehicle traveling down the road. What, Mara wondered, had seemed so magical about a family homestead in Mac's conversation.

Seals popped on Sammy's syrup as Mara came in. Sammy sat on her ring, smoking another cigarette. "You'll have to excuse my trips to the bathroom. I've had a number of stomach problems in recent years," she began. Sammy regaled Mara with accounts of vague back problems that developed every winter, as they waited for the seeds beneath the snow. In her hospitalizations, she had traveled Montana widely. She'd seen to it that Mary Lou became a registered nurse, showing Mara a photograph of a little girl with blond, ringleted ponytails. Sammy recalled conversations with the medical staff about her condition in great detail. Her condition stumped the experts. It was, Sammy confided, hopeless.

At noon, Mac and his cousins and their uncle Tuff shouldered into the kitchen. Tuff switched on the radio, listening for grain prices. Mac smiled at Mara, who translated "Have you had enough of Sammy yet?" Mara and Sammy dished up eggs between layers of hotcakes, patties of sausage, and milk. They bustled about the kitchen, Sammy adding more grounds to the coffee.

Mara studied Tuff's face, recognizing Alice in his whiskery grin. She listened to the gruff economy of his conversation, Sammy's practiced replies, silently chewed food.

"You drive a truck?"

When no one else answered, Mara realized Tuff was talking to her, flirting with her, offering Mara a reprieve. "I don't know," she answered, her mouth constricted by the sweet, astringent syrup.

"We'll put it in second for ya. All you have to do is press the pedal."

"I'll do up those dishes," Sammy added, waving the stub of her little finger. "We'll clean those chickens tomorrow."

All three combines emptied into Mara's truck. She eased it then back out through the fence, turning it over to a cousin who would drive the grain to town. Mac circled around, offering Mara a ride. She climbed up into the dusty combine beside him. Mac pointed out that Tuff's combine was air-conditioned, quiet, with music inside. They began a round.

"He likes you," Mac hollered. Mara shrugged. She was more interested in Mac's reasons for taking a week from his flooring contracts. Harvest was hardly a vacation.

"A quick buck," Mac hollered over the engine.

Mara calculated Mac's percentage using the price she'd heard at noon. "There's more to it than that."

"Okay, I'm my mother's muscle." Mac grinned, as the combine idled. The blades churned, lifted, as Mara climbed down to pick a rock.

"But wouldn't she get her share anyway?" Mara hollered, as Mac put the combine in gear.

Mac nodded. "Legally."

Mara rode half-perched on the edge of Mac's seat, itching from the chaff, hypnotized by the hopper filling with grain. "What's gonna happen when Tuff dies?" Mara hollered. Mac stopped to let Mara pick another rock. As she climbed back into the cab, Mac seemed not to have heard. The earth itself spoke in a cloud of chaff. But after another round, Mac spat out a mouthful of tobacco and the name "Mary Lou."

Mara and Mac made several rounds in silence. Mac pondered how all his years of neat swaths could amount to less than some man's errant seed. Mara's eyes followed a drop of sweat to Mac's temple. She studied the slight movement there, as her head throbbed in the heat. They gave up all effort to speak.

Mac's dog bounded out to greet him as the crew rode in from the field. The faded jeans waved at Mara. She drank a beer, in her thirst realizing the purpose of the drink. She gathered the jeans and headed toward the house to help with supper.

"Mara!" Sammy exclaimed. "This is my daughter, Mary Lou."

Mara nodded, seeing that supper was already on the table, the accountant waiting for the field hands to dig in to the beans. During the meal, Mara studied the heavy blond daughter, looking for the little girl in the photograph. She watched Tuff turn suddenly shy as Mary Lou asked him to pass the mashed potatoes. Mara excused herself. She played with the kittens in the bunkhouse for ten tired minutes before dark.

Mara wondered if Mary Lou knew she was adopted, as she picked feathers and washed innards the next morning. Each cousin believes he will one day own a piece of this homestead. Mara rinsed a gizzard. Hard way of life, look what it does to people.

"Mara," Sammy interrupted, "what are you thinking? Gotta take the stones out of those gizzards."

"Oh, that he must be a difficult man to live with."

Sammy smiled and nodded.

"That he loves Mary Lou dearly."

Sammy nodded again.

"That you're cleaning chickens so he can save it all up for her."

Sammy shoved a chicken into a milk carton for freezing. "I lost this little finger cleaning chickens."

"What about the cousins?" Mara asked, thinking of Mac.

Sammy studied the sky. "We'll take 'em lunch in the field."

Playing House

Gradually, Mac moved into one of his mother's basement apartments. He did so under pressure from Mara to make love. Mara stocked the old icebox with beer and snacks and made up a bed in the back room. A friend had given the couple a set of designer sheets for Christmas. Mara spread these across the mattress without a wrinkle, then a Hudson Bay blanket, a worn chenille spread, and an elk robe. On the dressing table, Mara placed a candle and lit it in midafternoon, liking its reflection off the mirror and the low, dark ceilings. Overhead, she could hear the creaking weight of his mother's body.

Then, because Mac said they could not make love without music, Mara set up Mac's stereo. When he lost his job, she hooked up the television. He lay all afternoon on the old hide-a-bed and watched soap operas. While Mara built bookshelves of bricks and boards, Mac set up his rifle rack. She bought more groceries and began to prepare meals of the elk and geese and fish he brought home, on a little gas oven without a thermostat. Before Alice knew it, the couple was comfortably settled in the apartment Mr. and Mrs. Wildman had vacated. The first month, instead of paying rent, they invited Alice to dinner. The meal would have been tasteless if it had not been burnt. Alice disapproved of their arrangement, but did not know what to do. She offered Mara the use of any kitchen utensil she might need.

So Mara helped herself to the candy thermometer permanently, washed their clothes, working around the clutter in Alice's laundry room. Mac stored his hunting equipment in the second basement apartment: his bows and arrows, reloading equipment, and a trunk of ammunition Mara could not lift. The couple passed evenings playing cards, tying flies and tip-ups, sewing leather patches on their jeans.

Mara became bored with the soap operas and the bad back that developed as a result of so much lying around. She changed the channel, read voraciously, and took a job at the little tavern where Mac played poker on Friday nights. Tips in chips from drunken millionaire ranchers in the back room made the job worthwhile. The coins collected first in Mara's cleavage, then in a big restaurant-sized pickle jar Mara kept under the kitchen sink. From time to time, Mara loaned Mac poker money from this jar.

They passed one winter in this way.

Ice Fishing

Mac drove seventeen miles east into the sunrise. The light was
warm coming through the window, but it was cold out, 30
below. Mara could see their breath inside Mac's van though
the heater ran full tilt. They searched the radio for a station
that played music instead of sermons. They settled for jazz
from some town in British Columbia they'd never heard of
before. Mara loved the music, went real well somehow with
that landscape out there. Deceptively simple. High, wide blue
sky. Prairie covered with snow. It was glacial land, rounded
and contoured, with huge rocks where no man would have left
one. Snow softened the contours. Behind the barbed-wire
fence, the expanse of white was untrampled as far as the eye
could see. Here and there, grass stuck through a foot of snow.
Sunlight refracted off snowflakes and gleamed. The light bent
in every direction. Mara sucked in her breath.

.   .   .

The van turned off on a little gravel road. A snowy owl on a pole swiveled its head toward the vehicle. The van drove along the shoreline of Nelson Reservoir, looking for a gentle incline. It turned again and Mara gasped as it drove out onto the lake.

The first time Mara didn't know that a lake this size, frozen over only three inches, could support a locomotive. That's what old-timers said. She gripped the door handle and Mac's friends in the back of the van laughed at her concern. The ice was ten inches thick. The van picked up speed. Mara could hear the wind howl around it. No road guided the van. Mac braked and the van spun in a perfect circle. Everyone laughed but Mara. The van picked up speed again, winding all over the lake. Later, Mara would understand there were faults in the ice. It was possible to go in, if a person couldn't recognize the crack. If you went fast and didn't look, the next thing you knew there'd be bubbles and fish floating before your eyes and cold dark liquid seeping in round your feet. You'd be in a panic with the door handle, letting yourself out into the liquid.

As the van slowed, Mara could hear the ice creak and complain beneath its wheels. The entire group piled out and shivered, making a plan. The men extended their arms and pointed out spots to drill holes. The wind unwound Mara's scarf. She fought with it, while the men drilled a semicircle of holes twenty-five yards apart with a gas-powered auger. Mara unwound the tip-ups, fifty-pound-test fishing line attached to small crosses of wood. The brave ones among the fishermen dipped a hand into the minnow bucket. It was impossible to hold on to the squirming minnows with mittens on. It was terribly cold to take the mittens off. The wind froze the skim of moisture from the bucket dry on their hands. Mac showed Mara how to put a hook through the minnow, twice for good measure. Still wiggling, they'd lower the minnows into the water. They lay the wooden crosses down across the holes.

Giant pike, walleye and northern, cruised in the dark waters beneath the ice, beneath their feet. The pike ate any fish smaller than themselves, the wiggling minnows. If they'd go for the minnows, if the hook caught them, the small cross "tipped up." Mac would lay his cribbage hand down on the dashboard and run to check the line. Sometimes the fish got away with the minnow or a part of a minnow. Mac would pull the line out and rebait it, the hooks catching on his cold hands. Other times, there'd be a fish wiggling on the end. He'd shout and throw a fist into the air. He'd dig the hook out of its mouth with a pair of pliers. Pike, especially northern, have wicked teeth. They can bite off the end of a finger. Mac would leave his catch on the ice, flopping their fins and trying to breathe air with their gills. Little by little, the fish froze. In the evening, Mac and Mara gathered them up and took them home.

Pike are better eating than trout. The flesh is flaky and the bones are fine enough to chew. There's nothing better than twitching pike in the frying pan, not even brook trout over a camp fire.

Mara was fascinated by Mac's huge hand around a filet knife, slicing this delicate flesh from the bone. She'd had him teach her how to clean. Mara would get out the cutting board and set to work. Sometimes, there were so many to clean, the fish began to thaw before Mara could finish. Then they'd begin to flop, some so vigorously Mara thought they'd flop out on the floor. Sometimes their tails would slap the cutting board. She'd have run her knife all down one side of the spine, flipping the filet back to run the knife between the flesh and the skin, and its mouth would move. Mara would scream and Mac would come to her rescue, smiling as he gave each slimy fish a good whack on its head with his pliers.

Mara dipped the filets in eggs and milk, corn meal and flour. A good batter.

Next morning, they got up early and checked the lines they'd left out overnight. They had to do this early, before other fishermen checked the lines for them. First, Mac checked the traps in the creek for more minnows, then followed the creek back toward the lake. Out of twenty-five lines, fifteen might have tipped up overnight. Overnight, the water froze around the line half an inch thick. Mara broke this skim of ice out with the toe of her boot. You couldn't just yank the fish out, you might lose him. Mac scooped the chunks of ice out with his bare hand. Mara couldn't stand to stick her hand in the water. For some reason, pulling it out of the water, back out into that dry, cold air nauseated her. Every time he'd do it, Mara studied the crosshatch on his skin. The texture of the skin magnified. She admired Mac for his ability to put his hand into a wet, icy hole. She couldn't understand why he didn't seem to feel the cold.

It never seemed quite fair, getting all those fish overnight for nothing, no work. After they'd checked and rebaited their lines, Mac and Mara spent the morning driving around seeing what kind of luck other fishermen were having. The fishermen would pass a flask back and forth between themselves, wipe their mouths, smack their lips, and lie to one another. Gradually Mara began to feel comfortable with the dark holes and vehicles parked all over the thin ice. She developed a reverence for those spots where men in vehicles had gone into the lake.

One day, Mac and Mara stayed out all day, playing cards and drinking. Mara was having a good day of cards and Mac persisted, wanting to win. They drank brandy in their coffee and laughed. The sun set before they knew it.

Mac decided they'd better check the lines one last time before heading home. He pulled the lines and Mara baited them. Even dressed like a sack of potatoes in all-weather coveralls, Mara complained of the cold. He warned her in country like this with temperatures below zero and a wind coming up, you'd get wind chills 30, maybe 40 below. Human beings couldn't last half an hour in weather like that. He told her to get in the van, to start the motor.

While Mac worked, Mara listened to the radio. Country western. He must have been out in the cold twenty minutes before he climbed in. Mac put the van in gear, circled. He ran the headlights all around them, looking for the spot they'd driven onto the lake. To Mara's eyes the horizon had disappeared. Mac drove in one direction, then changed his mind. He tried another. In a third direction, they saw the dark outline of a cabin and headed toward it. The bank there was too steep; they couldn't make the run from ice to land though they tried several times. Mara didn't worry, she trusted Mac.

Mac asked Mara to get out, put sand under the wheels. That didn't work. They tried boards. That didn't work. They wore a path in the ice with all their attempts to drive off the lake. Mac even had Mara push, to rock the van out of its rut. There was no traction. Mara's feet kept slipping out from under her. Nose to ice, nose to ice.

With a combination of these efforts, they eased the van out of position enough to take one last concentrated run for shore. The back wheels spun on the ice. Mara heard small cracklings. Wearily, she got out to push again. She felt the van take a bump and pull up over the bank.

Mara rode back to town with her hand on Mac's knee, by the light of the radio dial. There was a big white hole in the sky and the sound of fish flopping in the rear of the van.

A Landscape

Mara waited at an intersection. The light was red. Blue music circled the interior of the car. A black man, standing at a bus stop, suddenly smiled. The smile split the night into circles of unfocused color.

The light changed. Mara pressed the accelerator. Where had she felt this before? Somewhere south of the Milk River? The infinite stare of a coyote pup caught in the headlights? Or daylight? Dull, dun-colored prairie as far as her eye could see. An antelope moved. It seemed to have sensed her sight with its nose and fled into the horizon, white tail flapping over its rump. The prairie had broken into a thousand subtle colors. Mac had taught her to see these things.

Mara switched on the windshield wipers. No, more than that. South of the Milk River, but winter. The dog had scared up a jackrabbit. Its quick footprints. The flat landscape fattened, filled with rabbits. Rabbits whitened and brought to an abrupt red halt. Their warm stains wetting the snow. The hound whimpering in its dog dreams. Its legs twitching after the dream.

Dreaming, even as the highway pulled them 70 mph, east through a Sunday morning. Stubble stuck up through the snow, the sun high in a big sky. Each snowflake had reflected the sun. How could she have captured the colors, the contours? Outside the Art Institute, a statue stood. An ebony nude. A woman, several months pregnant, dripping in the rain.

On the radio that morning. Jazz. The music had held them in place, the place crammed with the past, that moment and the destination, drawn out over the future. All Mara had been able to do was breathe it in, breathe it out, see the breath congeal and watch its warmth dissolve on the window.

The dog lay between them, brooding, his skin loose along the floor. Mara's hand itched to scratch the dog to life again. She shifted. The dog was as unconscious as Mara was conscious of his muscles. It was as though he existed for the sheer purpose of beauty alone, to chase birds through the sky on all fours.

Once, in August, she'd seen his ear flap along the ripe heads of wheat. It had been a frantic attempt to keep pace with a cloud of dust the dog knew must be Mac's van. The ears gave the illusion of crippled wings, unable to rise. A seagull rising from water, the wheat had seemed like water. Nothing had seemed like what it was that August. A saxophone squealed. Mara's apartment building pulled into view.

How to Fry an Egg

In Hogeland, Montana, the view goes on for miles. In the summer, it's golden. Combines circle the fields, dying dogs circle the one intersection in town, flies buzz over the pile of beer cans behind the bar. That's where Jack parked Mara's kitchen. Inside her mobile home, Mara cooked for Jack and Mac and a crew of high school boys.

She opened the door and set a jar of clear water and tea bags on the step. A smell of vinegar wafted up her nose. Nine o'clock and already it was hot. With the back of her wrist, Mara brushed a wisp of hair out of her eyes. She'd just finished the breakfast dishes—eggy plates, juice glasses with pulp clinging to the sides, coffee cups full of rings. The sink in the trailer was twelve inches by eighteen and doing dishes was a chore.

It was her habit to spend the next two hours reading or writing letters. But this morning, Mara couldn't concentrate. She stared out the window at storm clouds gathering on the

Canadian border. She heard the *rat-tat-tat* of power wrenches at the construction site. The crew was building a granary, rings of corrugated steel they jacked up and jacked up until the granary towered nearly fifty feet in the air. Mara listened to a fly circle the inside of her cubicle. She had no appetite for her usual cup of coffee or cigarette.

Mara knew. She worried. She could not go to the doctor in Malta. It was a small town and she'd listened to enough of Alice's hospital gossip to know her secret could not keep. This knot in Mara's belly could be Alice's first grandchild.

Thursday, Jack drove to Havre for supplies—carpenters belts and bolts. Mara had him drop her off at a shaded clinic on Main Street long enough to make an appointment. Mara told the nurse she would take any doctor she could get that afternoon. The nurse ran the silver clicker of her ballpoint up and down the page of the appointment book. The phone rang and the receptionist went to answer. Mara drummed her fingers impatiently on the counter top. The receptionist returned and in a blue scrawl wrote out "Dr. Mayer, 4.30."

It was noon. The pickup idled across the street from the clinic. Mac grinned at Mara as she approached the dusty pickup. "What are you smiling about?" Mara asked, climbing in.

"I didn't recognize you," Mac admitted, continuing to ogle secretaries as they backed into noon hour traffic and made their way through town to the hardware store.

The errand took less time than making Mara's appointment had. They'd driven seventy miles for minutes' worth of supplies, but neither Jack nor Mac seemed upset that the late hour of Mara's appointment would cost them an afternoon's work. They decided to while away the afternoon in a tavern, the one they'd seen with the red vinyl-upholstered door. Jack ordered three beers.

The clientele was mostly Indian, so they sat aloof at one end of the bar. They put fifty-cent pieces in the jukebox, not daring to play pinball or lay a quarter on the pool table. Mara sat quietly, nursing her morning sickness into the afternoon. The banter between Mac and Jack dwindled. Mac said he thought he'd go buy a pair of bootlaces. Mara sat up straight on her stool, struggling out of her preoccupation to ask Jack questions about his wife's pregnancy, how it was for her. Melanie was due any day, but Jack couldn't answer Mara's questions. He hadn't been home longer than to repack his suitcase in months.

"I've been cut off," he said, laughing his big Swede's lippy laugh. When Mara didn't laugh, he said, "You're worried, aren't you?" She nodded, shrugged her shoulders, and looked at the clock. Twelve minutes to four. Mara lit one last cigarette and tapped her foot as Jack stacked change on the counter. The barmaid came and collected their empties. She asked, "Another?"

Jack nodded and Mara shook her head. Mac wasn't back. No parting kiss as Mara climbed off the stool and stepped across the threshold into daylight. She blinked, looked up and down the street. No bearded figure, no man with a small sack of bootlaces making his way up either side of the street. Not even a place where you could buy bootlaces. Mara walked to the corner and crossed with the light.

With a great effort to walk a straight line, Mara walked the block and a half to the clinic. Cool, color-coordinated interior. Magazines. The receptionist looked up without recognition. Her hairdo had come undone. "Dr. Mayer? Oh yes, Miss Johnson. He'll be right with you."

Mara had leafed as far as the People section of *Time* magazine when a nurse carrying a file called Mara's name and said, "Follow me."

Mara sat clothed, waiting in Dr. Mayer's huge office. The chair she sat in was a practical, straight-backed wooden one like Mara remembered from grade school. She studied the clutter on his desk, the prescription pad and insurance forms, topped with a stethoscope. She had her head tilted to read the title of a medical book when the door opened and an old man stepped into the room. "Now, what seems to be the problem?"

Dr. Mayer's white coat came to his knees. By the gray halo of hair and the tired four o'clock eyes behind his wire-rimmed glasses, Mara estimated his age as a month or two short of retirement. He sat in the squeaky desk chair and revolved around to face Mara. She licked her lips, wiped her nose on the back of her hand. The doctor handed his patient a Kleenex.

"I wonder if I'm pregnant."

"What makes you think so?"

"Well, I haven't bled. I'm two weeks overdue. My breasts ache." Mara squirmed in her T-shirt. "I'm nauseated in the morning. Could you take a urine sample?"

"Could, but it's too soon to tell that way."

Mara sniffed again, not needing to.

"Is there some way to find out?"

The doctor drew out a long yes and asked Mara if she was married.

"No."

"What will you do?"

"Get rid of it."

"How?"

"Abortion."

"What makes you think that's a solution?"

"The father doesn't want it and I don't want it. We're children ourselves. Neither of us wants the responsibility."

Dr. Mayer cleared his throat. "Do you use birth control?"

Mara shook her head, not bothering to explain her problems with pills and IUDs—how the pills had made her bleed thirty days out of the month, or how her body had rejected two IUDs. And she could not recall the name of the gynecologist, only that of the clinic she'd gone to in Missoula.

"Abortion, young lady, is not a form of birth control."

The man rose from his desk, asking Mara to undress. He'd be back.

Mara skinned off her tight jeans and T-shirt. Her breasts felt like ripe fruit. A thick mucus stained the crotch of her panties.

Dr. Mayer returned with his nurse. Firmly, he told Mara to lie back and draw up her legs. He stood between her bent knees thumping Mara's belly with two fingers. He sighed and sat down, pulling a small spotlight into position over his head. His old gleaming head shook, but Mara could not tell if it was from age or attitude.

The doctor spread a lubricant on Mara's genitals and roughly inserted two fingers. Mara felt the fingers move every which way and she hated her reliance on this man. As the doctor withdrew his hand, an unidentified mucus dribbled out of Mara's body onto the textured paper toweling of his examining table.

The doctor spat into Mara's glistening crotch.

He asked his nurse for a Kleenex. Dutifully, she handed
him one. Roughly, he wiped the dribble away. He turned his
broad, bent back on Mara. He wrote in the file.

The nurse followed Dr. Mayer from the room and Mara
dressed, still not knowing. She sat again in the school chair
by his desk, a Kleenex balled up in her hand. Mara watched
the clock tick slowly toward 4:47. A rough turn of the doorknob broke her fascination with the second hand.

Dr. Mayer shuffled across the room and collapsed into his
chair. Tilting back, he stared hard into Mara's face. He nodded
his head.

Mara asked that the results be sent to Missoula as she made
out her check. The Women's Clinic there would point her in
the right direction. She and Mac could stay with Lane or Rick.
Turning away from the counter, Mara looked at the sunlight
on the other side of the entrance to this dim waiting room.
Her vision blurred. Trees swam into cars swam into traffic
into buildings. Mara made her way back to the bar without
a false step.

It was happy hour when Mara arrived. The number of customers had multiplied. One let out a whoop as Mara's eyes
adjusted to the darkness of the place. The customer caught
himself when Mara joined Jack at the bar. Mac was in the
men's room. They'd switched from beer to whiskey ditches.
Mara ordered herself two and threw a twenty at the barmaid.

"Well, what's the verdict?"

Mara turned slowly on her stool to stare at the figure settling
in beside her. "What took you so long?"

Jack hurried away to the men's room. Mara and Mac stared
at one another, each waiting for a reply. At length, Mac said,
"I bumped into Mary Lou."

"And?"

"If the weather holds, they'll start cutting any day."

Mara finished her drink, chewed an ice cube. She slurred, "You have a prior commitment."

Mac sipped at Mara's second drink, the whiskey burning one thought into his mind: he'd show the Mary Lous they couldn't cheat him out of his property. "To the homestead. What'll you do?"

Mara ordered more drinks. "Well," she said, studying the melt of ice cubes in her glass. "The first thing I'm gonna do is schedule a vasectomy for you. You've talked about it long enough. Now you know the damn thing works."

Mara looked Mac steadily in the eye. He said, "I knew that already."

Three Dreams

Mara dreamed she waited for a girl friend in a motel room, when an actual knock came to her apartment door. The knock was so insistent, Mara woke and stumbled to the door. It was 3 a.m. No sooner did she turn the knob than the weight of a drunk forced the door in on her. The drunk wore a fishing cap and had a huge nose. He kept asking for Marcia. Mara kept telling him, "You have the wrong door." Her robe gaped open. "Marcia, Marcia," the drunk said, reaching for Mara's breasts. They swung just out of his reach as Mara heaved the parts of his body over the threshold enough to close the door again.

Mac was fishing. Mara saw him disappear through a fault in the ice. His voice made a falling sound she mistook for "Help." She ran across the ice and peered down into the hole. The dark icy waters Mara expected to see had crystallized and formed a huge, brilliant room under the lake surface. There, Mara saw

Mac and his mother in a remote domestic scene. She called to
him and he answered, "I'm okay. Don't worry." She watched
his mother putter around. Alice apparently couldn't hear
Mara's voice. "It's okay," Mac said again, "I don't need you."

Mara dreamed she'd have the baby at home, with girl friends
attending. When the dream came, none of them knew what
to do. None of them knew how to hold its slick body. The
plucked, pimpled chicken slipped from their arms onto the
bed, fluid as a cat. It slithered over the edge of the bed. They
were horrified to hear it hit the floor. They scrambled to retrieve
it, to reassure it, but it snaked away. No sooner would one
of them close a fist around its long, slender body than it would
slide away. Another hand closed around it just behind the
head. Again, it slid away. While Mara's girl friends stared at
their empty fists, Mara herself seemed to get a firmer hold.
But the snake, this child of Mara's, turned to a fish and flipped
out of her hands onto the floor again. A mucus formed on its
scales. They tried to get hold of the baby. They tried to get
hold of themselves. It was Shelly, a friend Mara was yet to
meet, who accidentally stepped on the fish. Mara screamed,
hearing the tiny crush of its bones. Shelly lifted her foot,
revealing the distorted shape of an ant.

The girls stared at the spot, speechless. The floor creaked
and splintered as a tree sprouted through the hardwood. Visibly
it grew, lifting the ceiling with its boughs. It towered above
them. Its limbs filled the room.

PART II

Asking for a Hand

He first called during a dinner party Mara gave for several friends. They were having after-dinner drinks when the phone rang. She made it clear to him that it was neither the time nor the place to discuss such a thing. She unplugged her phone.

Then he began to call her at work. After several Saturdays of his interruptions, she told him he could come to Kansas City, discuss it on her territory, if he was serious. Mara returned to her paperwork, expecting never to hear from him again.

One Tuesday, he called asking Mara to meet him: 2:15 a.m. at the airport. Mara looked out the window at the snow dubiously. She had no way there except the last airport express bus at ten thirty, no way to be sure his plane could land after all her waiting.

She took a magazine with her and during the bus ride chatted with a man who told her he was a nightclub singer. The man was on his way to Denver, but he took Mara's false name and phone number anyway. Then, for four hours, Mara sat at the proper gate, reading in a chrome and vinyl sling of a chair. Red caps wandering by lazily glanced at Mara out of the corners of their bloodshot eyes. She smiled, enjoying the anonymity.

Mac's plane landed in a flurry of snowflakes. He was one of the last passengers to shuffle into the terminal. While Mara noted he'd been careful to tuck his flannel shirt into his jeans, his eyes uncomfortably studied the height of the terminal ceiling before they fell on Mara.

It had been nearly two years. Mac thought Mara had put on some weight and poked her in the side playfully. She smiled wanly. She'd worked all day, would have to work tomorrow. "I'm tired."

Together they stood at the luggage carousel, searching for things to say. Mara was first to spot his bag, though Mac grabbed it. He followed her out to the taxicab lane, watching the arm she flung out in the snow-filled air. They shared the expensive cab with a ragged-looking salesman who set his sample case on their feet. The cabbie slid his cab all over the highway and asked for a twenty when he pulled up at Mara's apartment building.

Mara's roommate was asleep on the couch when she and her guest arrived. Mac would have to share her bed.

When he woke, Mac didn't know where he was or who this woman was. The bed had jostled him into dreams of driving the combine or cross-country, hunting antelope. Gradually, the violence of the bedclothes, the chill in the room, brought him round. The body knelt over his, the flying head of hair, was Mara's as far as he could make out by the dim light along her venetian blinds.

She'd left him no directions, so Mara was surprised when Mac appeared punctually at her office for their lunch date. She took a good daylight look at him and decided they'd eat hamburgers and drink cold beers in the workingmen's bar across the street. As she told him they'd been invited to her parents' for supper that evening, Mac pulled a clear plastic bubble from his pocket. Wordlessly, he handed the bubble to Mara. She grinned and slipped the twenty-five-cent engagement ring on the third finger of her right hand.

Mara's father picked them up at 38th and Main, a corner famous for streetwalkers, on his way home from work. He strained to keep the conversation going the eighteen miles down Main, Troost, the Paseo, toward the suburbs. They were miles Mara thought she could drive blindfolded. Finally, Mr. Johnson tuned in a middle-of-the-road FM station. The trio rode in silence, Mara wondering if the one man's reticence attracted her to the other. The engagement ring flashed in the car's dark interior.

It was a relief to pull up before the house on the hill in Skyline Heights. It looked like many other houses in the neighborhood, but the familiar swing of her father's Buick off the hill into the driveway made it home. The house was alive with lights and music. As they climbed the steps, Mara could hear her mother's laughter, smell lasagna cooking.

Mara had not known there were other guests coming for supper. Immediately coming into the house, she heard Sam Miller's laugh. He and his wife, Marion, were neighbors. She understood why her mother had invited them, to keep the conversation rolling. Though Sam worked for the post office, he'd killed a few birds in his time. Hunting would keep the dinner conversation light.

Mr. Johnson took Mac's down jacket with a rustle. Mac stood in the entryway awkwardly until Mara's mother offered him a drink.

"Scotch."

Mara twisted the stone of her bauble around to the inside of her hand and went to help the women making salad in the kitchen. She sipped wine from a tumbler.

By the time they sat down to eat, Mara was giddy. She felt closed off from her parents and the Millers, in a private joke with Mac. Mac, on the other hand, tried valiantly to include himself in the conversation. The Bob Marshall wilderness? He knew it like the back of his hand, he boasted. The ring twisted round and round on Mara's finger, to the candlelit clatter of silverware.

At last, when their plates were smears of tomato sauce, the Millers rose to go. "Another day, another dollar," Sam always said. After lingering good-byes at the door, Mara's father retreated downstairs in the direction of his study. She heard the ice in Mac's fourth Scotch clink, heard him follow her father down the stairs.

Mara helped her mother clear the table. "Did you notice the ring?"

"Yes."

Mara laughed. "He bought it out of a bubblegum machine." She laughed again.

"But you're wearing it on the right hand. None of us knew what to think."

Mara blushed. She hadn't realized the mistake.

"Have you reached a decision?"

"We haven't even talked about it yet. Just this ring." Mara continued to wipe the plates dry. "Says his uncle needs him to manage the family homestead."

Mara studied the few suds that floated on the gray dishwater. She could see neither of her mother's hands as she scrubbed at the silverware.

"Is that what you want?"

Mara shrugged. Staring at her mother's raw, red hands, Mara pondered the question. *Do you want to be a farm wife? Kill chickens and throw bales and let your breasts droop to your waist? Do you want to give up your good job and lovely apartment and all your friends?* Likening the lines of Montana prairie to the museum spareness of the apartment she shared with Dennis, Mara couldn't answer. Her father came up the stairs. Two ice cubes rattled in the bottom of his glass.

"You ready to head back into town?"

"Guess so." Mara folded her towel as Mac emerged from the bowels of the Johnsons' split-level house. It was a moment of recognition. Mac was a stranger, a character out of her past. Two years past. She studied him by the harsh overhead light of her mother's kitchen.

They lay in Mara's bed, listening to Dennis turn the pages of his book. Mac said, "I talked to your father."

"About what?"

"Us."

"What about us?"

"I asked him if I could marry you."

Mara stifled a laugh. "I'm touched, but what an old-fashioned thing to do." She rolled over to face him, touched his shoulder. Once she could no longer hear the pages of her roommate's book turning down the hallway and she thought Mac was asleep, she said, "What did he say?"

A voice in the dark answered, saying, "It's up to you."

Each day of his visit, Mara worked. Mac lay on the sofa, reading books Mara suggested. Little by little, the trailer they would occupy at the homestead became a little log cabin in the woods, with blue skies and a few prearranged, fluffy clouds. Mac would trap and Mara would garden and they would live off the land.

Privately, Mac wanted to know how it was that Dennis escorted a different beautiful woman each night of the week. Mara wondered about his uncle's health and just what Mary Lou's husband was doing these days. Instead, they talked about the cabin over sloppy beers at the workingmen's bar. As the sun set between the cramped apartment buildings in her neighborhood, the leafless trees seemed to claw at Mara's window, wanting in. Though Mara never said yes, she'd never said no.

Mac caught the airport express at a luxury hotel on the Plaza. The bus idled as executives piled on in all-weather coats and briefcases. Mac in his flannel shirt bent to kiss Mara's lips. For a moment he watched the snow fall around her face and melt on the heated sidewalk. A black man with shiny brass buttons across his chest appeared, clapping his gloved hands mutely. Mac stepped up onto the idling bus. Its doors folded, closed, behind him.

Once the bus pulled away, Mara bought a *New York Times*. She ordered a croissant in the hotel coffee shop. She left the ring in the ashtray.

Dennis' Wrist

Mara's roommate was a secretary named Dennis. Their arrangement, sharing an old luxury apartment in what had become a bad part of Kansas City, had worked well. A long hallway connected three bedrooms; Dennis said it reminded him of railroad apartments in New York. The high ceilings and spacious dimensions dwarfed their few pieces of furniture. The apartment reminded Mara of eastern Montana, while Dennis referred to it as "minimalist." The apartment was more than either of them could have afforded alone. Splitting the rent, they kept separate bedrooms, telephones, and schedules. When Mara listened to helicopters patrol her street at night, she liked the idea of having a man around the house.

Dennis packed Mara's books into cardboard boxes for her move north. He mumbled something about a woman's touch. Mara, dismantling the bricks and boards, said "What's that?" The words echoed in the emptying room, the middle bedroom they called the library.

"Let's celebrate tonight."

Matter-of-factly, Mara agreed.

Dennis made reservations at a small family restaurant that didn't take reservations. An Italian place in the Italian part of town. They overdressed. Mara wore a white linen suit—a slim skirt and blazer, with a sheer mauve blouse she knew she would have no more occasion to wear. He wore baby blue and light gray. They sweat, elegantly anyway, in traffic as they searched for Tony's.

Inside, Tony's looked much like Montana truck stops. The unfinished edges of paneling particularly brought truck stops to mind. The chrome chairs and vinyl upholstery reminded Dennis of the diners he'd been so fond of in Manhattan. One table was set for a party of twenty, and couples kept drifting in dressed in jeans, baseball jerseys and caps. They ordered beers and made toasts and sang raucous songs as Dennis and Mara's drinks went watery. Both Dennis and Mara shivered in the air-conditioned air.

Dennis looked up. A candle, flickering in a red glass net-covered jar, illuminated his face. His Scandinavian features said, "They're famous for their fried chicken." So that's what Mara ordered, without realizing all a Tony's chicken dinner entailed. Waiting, they drew shapes on the checked tablecloth and discovered wads of dried gum under the tabletop as they crossed their legs. The waitress brought a relish tray and watery salads and a basket of rolls and a hot plate of crisp golden chicken with mashed potatoes and a hearty gravy. And a side of spaghetti. Dennis and Mara's mouths moved and moved. Bones littered their plates. The waitress took the plates away, then brought half a spiked watermelon and two long straws. To the other table, she carried a chocolate cake with sparklers.

"Happy birthday to you, happy birthday to you." Mara listened to them sing. The plump women in tight jeans began to fall over the men and paper noisemakers unrolled and rolled and unrolled. The watermelon loosened Mara's tongue. She said nonsense things. She told Dennis he was beautiful and Dennis replied, "You should never have to be seen with a man who isn't." And then he began to sing all the old romantic songs that made Mara move in with him in the first place. "Blue skies, shining at me, nothing but blue skies do I see."

But it was a clear dark night. They stood on their apartment building's tiny lawn and admired a ring around the full moon. Dennis' shadow beside Mara's was tall as a skyscraper. Skyscrapers and newspapers blowing along empty city streets and the 1940s. "I've got a headache."

Mara went in for an aspirin. She kicked off her heels and padded down the hall in her stockinged feet to Dennis' room. His mattress lay centered on his bedroom floor. His room was surrounded by windows. The shifting shadows of trees in the thick air behind the shades was Bergmanesque, they decided. They could hear the ivy climb the walls, the clock tick.

Mara kneeled on the slick hardwood floor beside the bed. She'd been in this bed. Together, she and Dennis had rolled around like brother and sister, naked and laughing. Dennis folded his trousers along the crease, hung them particularly on a hanger. He straightened his twisted sheets with one big billow and climbed in. He punched the pillow into shape. Drowsily, he began to mumble all the things people are supposed to say when they part.

Mara held one hand but felt Dennis' wrist go limp, and

letting go the hand, she watched it hang from the edge of the bed. All Mara wanted to tell him was that she'd seen the rough immigrant angle of his wrist as he washed vegetables at their kitchen sink. Mara was about to say "You don't fool me," and her lips were parted, when Dennis began to snore.

The Prodigal's Father

Mac, packing boxes of books down two flights of stairs, complained they weighed nearly as much as his guns. Mara
laughed, insincerely it seemed to Mac, and took a swig from
her beer. The air was thick with insects and humidity. Sweat
soaked into the ribs of Mac's undershirt as he worked to load
his van with Mara's belongings.

He drank a beer as they drove toward the suburbs. City
traffic irritated him. Up north, he'd have covered sixty miles
rather than fifteen by the time they pulled into the Johnsons'
driveway.

Mrs. Johnson greeted Mac with another beer on the front
step. She fed the two of them her grilled, gourmet version of
catfish. She did not try to make conversation. It was obvious
to her that Mac was tired. Instead, she made up the bed in
the guest room, Mara's old room, then slipped off to sleep
herself.

Mac went upstairs to shower. For a few minutes, Mara sat
on the patio with her father. They watched fireflies and sucked

their cigarettes. Mara was listening to the locusts when her father stood, unexpectedly, and said good night.

"Good night?" Mara's voice trailed off into a question. This was so unlike him. She had expected a last-minute, philosophical discussion about marriage, at least some advice. She sat on the chaise longue thinking about this until the sky grew dark as the houses around her. Then, she felt her own way upstairs to bed. Mac was already asleep.

The bed was very likely the one Mara had been conceived in. It had been handed down to Mara and her sister years ago because of a depression in the middle. Her parents had since slept in a spacious king-size bed. Mara and Mac kept rolling together and pulling apart. The air was too sticky to touch.

Mara lay in the dark, blinking. It really wasn't very dark. A yard light across the street shone in the bedroom window. It had ever since Mara was a little girl. It illuminated things like a full moon. In fact, she often mistook it for a full moon. She felt safe and singled out because this moon deigned to shine in her room.

The next thing Mara knew, it was morning. By the time she woke, her mother had left for work. Her father lingered over his newspaper and coffee longer than usual. They exchanged pleasantries, but Mac was anxious to be on the road.

Mara's father walked out to the van; rather, he followed her out. He was barefoot and it was still chilly. The grass was long, each blade distinct for Mara. It covered her father's feet. He had on his inevitable trousers and a ribbed undershirt. His hands were in his pockets, his elbows close to his sides, keeping him warm.

The birds were oblivious, sweet and dumb in the Johnsons' two elm trees. Mara got in and slammed the van door. She made some joke about her belongings. She looked out through the windshield and then turned to look at her father through the passenger's window. Their eyes traveled all over each other's faces. A long, silent searching look. Mac cleared his throat. Mara slowly rolled her window down.

She expected her father to say "Don't go." But he was at a loss for words. Mac broke their hypnosis, easing the van away from the curb. Mara didn't look back. Her eyes watered a little, winding through town toward the highway. She and Mac traded observations: Isn't the sky in Missouri a paler shade of blue? Mac nodded glumly. Exhaust from industrial smoke-stacks along the river trailed slowly through the sky. "Can you believe it's the same river?" Mac looked at the sluggish Missouri. His stretch of the same river, fifty miles south of home, was a wilderness area, with little skips of white water. Ancient paddlefish cruised the crumbling castles of the Breaks, even the antelope paused to look down into the mountain range that had once been underwater. Mac thought of the twisted scrub pine that grew there. He pressed the accelerator. The van responded sluggishly.

"Is something wrong?" Mara asked, turning from the land-scape to Mac.

Mac shook his head no.

"Isn't it green here?" And Mac nodded, pulling away from the midwest in April.

Wall Drug

Mara studied the map. If they went across Nebraska, then up
through South Dakota, she reasoned, the drive would be more
interesting and they wouldn't have to deal with Denver after
all of Kansas. She drew a dark line from the dreary little
Nebraska town where they sat in a cafe eating salads left over
from lunch to Wall, South Dakota, through Blackjack and
past Custer's battlefield into the southeastern tip of Montana.

Mac paid for their meal and went to gas up the van, while
Mara disappeared into the ladies' room. As Mara dried her
hands, she read the graffiti on the walls. "But I just assumed
you had a vasectomy," and "Toxic shock syndrome has finally
given women something intelligent to scribble on rest room
walls." She smiled and described the lines to Mac as they drove
several miles down the wrong highway. He noticed it first.
The road signs were wrong. The sun was going down and the
weather worsening. Suddenly, Mac turned off onto a country
road, driving due north.

Mara trusted his sense of direction though there were fewer signs along this road than the last. As they came over a small rise, the asphalt suddenly turned to dirt. Mara got out the map and studied it again.

"Reservation. Must be," Mac said.

Mara put her finger on Rosebud, South Dakota. "Probably."

The rain they'd left in Nebraska turned to a fine, freezing mist. As they jostled over unkempt roads, Mara heard her grandmother's antique dresser crash into her guitar. The mist thickened to snowfall.

It was late April, but this was blizzard nevertheless. The road began to wind and the sky darken and though Mac drove with his headlights on bright, there were no signs to be seen. "Lock your door."

Mara did as she was told, but looked at Mac questioningly. Off to the left, she saw a man stumbling along the ditch. "Let's give him a lift. Maybe he can give us directions."

Mac cast a look at the back of the van. It was packed to capacity with Mara's belongings. "He's drunk. Indian."

Mara rode in silence, in some danger she didn't understand. Twenty miles later, the van passed through a community of tumbledown houses. Mara saw no one on the streets, though there were lights in the windows. Again, Mara suggested they stop for directions.

Mac drove on without a word, his jaw set firmly, but obscurely in his beard. Forty-five minutes later they came to a junction and stopped. Snowflakes flew hypnotically into their headlights. Mac allowed Mara to get out and peer at the number on the sign. Once he'd located the spot on the map, he got out and peed.

. . .

They stayed at the first motel that would take Mara's credit card. And they laughed the next morning over nickel coffee and cafeteria hotcakes at how many Wall Drug signs they must have missed shortcutting through the reservation. Mara had counted eighty along the highway before they'd stopped for breakfast. The place was an obvious tourist trap, though quiet this morning after a blizzard. Mac was anxious to move on. He'd seen two semis slip off the slick highway into the median. He was having trouble making out any sort of horizon. Mara could only fondle the postcards and gaudy turquoise as they passed through the gift shop after their meal.

She wondered aloud if Wall Drug ever filled a prescription. Mac didn't laugh. She tried to describe a decor of tourist kitsch to him, but he still didn't smile as the van pulled out on the highway behind a sand truck.

In picture postcards Mara mailed home, she described how at Mount Rushmore George Washington's nose ran that day, as Mac photographed the bellies of birds circling overhead. From Deadwood, South Dakota, she wrote: "Here, Wild Bill Hickok was shot in the back of the head, playing poker. He held a hand of aces and eights. A deadman's hand."

Mac took a long sip of beer and tucked the can between his legs. He'd begun to narrate the trip with stories he'd read in western American history. Mara claimed she would be able to feel the moment they crossed the state line into Montana, whether it was marked or not. The sun shone for the first time in a thousand miles. The prairie was the same ahead of and behind the van. Mara became lost in all this landscape recalled to mind. She took one of their two remaining beers and lapsed into excited silence. Her blood felt carbonated.

She felt the van slow and turn off onto a gravel drive. "Where are we?" In the distance, Mara saw run-down ranches with beehives and swaybacked horses.

"Custer's Last Stand."

Curious, Mara sat up. The grass shivered in the breeze as far as her eye could see. Mac drove slower and slower, as if not to disturb the gravel. They mounted a low rise and stopped. Mara pointed out a tiny white wild flower that dotted the hillside. Mac pointed out several granite stones jutting at odd angles from the ground. Mara climbed out for a closer look, slowly realizing each stone marked a grave. The stones multiplied and surrounded her. Mara ran, counting like a child, until she lost track at 139.

Mac talked about the battle halfway across Montana. Mara watched the prairie begin to gather itself up into mountains. She welcomed the scent of pine after long hours of prairie wind moaning at the van's contours. They sped obscenely through the landscape, history, and many individual stories. Mara slumped with fatigue.

They began to see mileage signs—Missoula 200 miles, 89 miles. Then, "VD attacks one Montanan every hour." They rounded a mountain, took the first exit, and merged into late afternoon traffic. Several drivers waved a greeting to Mac, including a tanned girl in a low sports car. Mac stopped a block from Lane's shop and bought another cold six-pack.

Mac now lived with Lane in a bachelor apartment off his

taxidermy shop. The boys were all there, waiting for Mac. Mara nodded a greeting to those she knew, Lane and Rick, and excused herself. Her bladder was about to burst.

Rick had a new pistol he wanted Mac to try. They waited for Mara in Rick's car. "I'm tired," she said, climbing into the cramped backseat of Rick's sports car. "Couldn't this wait?"

Rick laughed the crazed laugh Mara thought she'd forgotten. The tires squealed as he backed out and darted through traffic. On the I-90 access road he cruised until sunset, drinking beer and shooting birds off power lines. Mac watched for gophers.

Mara saw it before Mac cried, "There's one." Rick handed him the pistol. He propped it out the car door and peered down the barrel, waiting for the gopher to peer out of its hole. Within seconds, it reappeared, looking curiously from side to side as if it smelled them. Mac shot. A direct hit. The gopher's tiny leg shivered with its last nervous reaction. Its head was gone.

Mara sat stunned, as Mac handed the pistol back to Rick. He grinned at his friend, glad Rick had finally found a gun he was comfortable with. Rick craned around to ask Mara, "You wanna try?"

Mara hadn't held a gun in two years. From her cramped quarters in the backseat, she could only shoot free hand. Hefting the gun, she scanned their surroundings for a target. Her eyes narrowed, focusing on a distant power pole the size of a matchstick. She followed the matchsticks back from infinity toward the car, squeezing the trigger, shattering the insulator of the first pole to loom large as a cross.

The Literal Smell of Death

A little bell over the door rang as Mara entered Valley Taxi-dermy. The entryway served as a trophy room. Heads of deer, elk, antelope, moose, sheep, and goat stuck rigidly out from the walls. A duck spread the wings of its stuffed body over a counter that separated the trophy room from the taxidermist's shop.

Lane peered over the counter from his workbench. An old smile spread across his face at the new arrival. "Mara!" Mac stepped into the shop behind her.

Mara gave Lane a wooden hug, looking over his shoulder at the disarray in the shop. Not much had changed. Tanned hides lay everywhere. Hides in various stages of skinning draped over several old dinette chairs. Tagged rack of deer, antelope, and elk hung from the rafters along with a pair of stretched bear skins. Forms for elk mounts jutted at odd angles from the floor. The walls were papered with *Playboy* center-folds. The false eyes Lane fitted into his mounts stared up from the clutter of tools on his workbench.

Mara vaguely remembered what the boys used to say about Lane. He was an "artist." He had a way of making your trophy look lifelike, the way he painted in around the eyes.

Lane and Mara stepped back from their hug, holding each other at arm's length. Deep lines fanned out into Lane's freckled, weathered skin from either sallow green eye.

"What's that smell?"

"Huh? Oh, I've been sawing this rack in half. Easier to handle. Bone."

Mac entered the shop again through the apartment door. Mara wandered off to the apartment. A bathroom connected the shop with the garage Lane and Mac were in the process of remodeling into living quarters.

The kitchen and living area surrounded a wood stove. And though there were boots and hats and hunting gear strewn everywhere, the room had a woman's touch. An afghan over the back of a dilapidated couch and a plant tied up to a stake. Off this big room, two hollow doors set in plasterboard walls led into the bedrooms. The first room Mara peered into she decided must be Mac's. She recognized the dresser under all the shotgun shells and .22 cartridges. One drawer would not close, it was so full of socks.

She carried her bags in herself. Mara cleared a spot on the floor to open her suitcase at a right angle to the wall. She dug several paperbacks out of the toilet items in her flight bag. Mara piled the books to one side of Mac's unmade bed and washed her face. Until they found a place of their own, Valley Taxidermy would do just fine.

The woman's touch did not belong to the wife of Lane's Mara had known, but to a big, friendly gal named Shelly. She'd made an arrangement similar to Mara's in Lane's bedroom. She'd lost thirty pounds over the summer at his urging. In the mornings when Mara went looking for something to eat, the cupboards were bare.

Mac would be away during the week, finishing a flooring contract for a convalescent center he said was built over a swamp. Shelly rushed off to a job at the university each morning at eight, and Lane busied himself in the shop. Mara rolled out of bed at ten, without an appetite. She'd drink a cup of coffee and read the paper, scanning the classifieds. Every day she'd make a few calls, write a letter, mail off an application. She took her time in the bathroom, matched up Mac's socks, read from her stockpile of paperbacks until Shelly came home from work. By five o'clock, Lane had usually disappeared. Mara and Shelly would sit over a bowl of peanuts and wonder where their men were.

In time, Mara began to think of Shelly's friendliness as naiveté. Mara was engaged to Mac; Shelly merely lived with Lane. Shelly gushed on about Lane this, Lane that. Mara did not tell her the "good old boy" stories she heard as customers came and went during the day. If Mara could believe what she heard through the bathroom door, the sounds Shelly supposed were mice in the attic had been Lane stuffing some woman named Debbie. Mara wanted to tell her friend the truth and didn't because they were friends. Most women, Mara thought, wised up in their own time.

Mac rolled out linoleum in the convalescent home through May and June, into July. Women stopped by the shop asking for him. Mara became disenchanted with sharing the bathroom with Lane's customers, the interruptions to her job search and her reading. The unidentified smell in the apartment on hot afternoons drove her out. She took walks along the train tracks.

On Friday afternoons, Mara made pitchers of fresh fruit dai-
quiris, so good even the boys made a point to be home. They
leaned up against the vehicles in Valley Taxidermy's parking
lot, sipping their drinks, swatting flies, and rating runners as
they passed.

Mara began to help Shelly pick up after the boys. The place
was clean, but flies proliferated in the apartment and the
unidentified smell hung in the air. Mara learned to coexist
with them. She learned to read without flinching at their
touch. She learned to like their quick, tiny touch as they
wandered among the hairs on her arm.

Mara did not begin to scan the classifieds for rentals until
one afternoon after Lane had shuffled through the apartment
to its back door. The unidentified smell poured into the room.
Mara left her book open over the back of the couch and went
to see what Lane was after. There, on a small enclosed patio,
maggots swarmed in and out of twenty-five assorted animal
skulls. Mara closed her eyes, still seeing the skulls crawl in a
thousand different directions. She swallowed the vomit that
rose in her throat.

Second Thoughts

Mac hoped one day to inherit the management of the family homestead. A second seizure had left his uncle Tuff confined to a wheelchair, drooling into a bib, dependent on Sammy and Mary Lou for every need. Sammy had hired a baby-sitter to tend the grandchildren, while Mary Lou tended to her father in the new house constructed to accommodate their medical needs. Sammy looked better than Mara had ever seen her.

The sky at the homestead was overcast. The cousins, gathered faithfully for harvest, drank beer in the quonset, the tension in the sky threatening to erupt between them. Mary Lou fed her father applesauce, though Tuff winked lecherously at Mara in recognition. She smiled and bowed her head.

Impatient with the weather, the uncle that refused to die, the houseful of women, Mac drove Mara to his mother's. The women could go ahead with wedding plans, while Mac's combine circled the fields. He'd promised Mara to think things over.

Mara thought things over sitting at the kitchen table, her elbows propped on Alice's crosswords. His mother had worked all night; she slept now. She'd sold the old boardinghouse and moved into a trailer on the edge of town. The wind howled around it. The sound made Mara shiver. She couldn't believe Alice could sleep through that sound, even after a hospital graveyard shift.

Wind chimes tinkled. Gauze curtains billowed. Cats slunk in and out and about Mara's ankles, Alice's houseplants. One cried, clinging to the screen door, and Mara let it out. The prairie unfurled endlessly from Alice's doorstep. A sense of timelessness paralyzed Mara; Grandma Winter's rocker moved within it, with it.

"You're a dull bride-to-be." Alice's voice surprised Mara around noon. Mara sat at the kitchen table where Alice had left her four hours before. Mara shrugged. She'd redone Alice's crosswords and begun to read. Her breasts ached.

After lunch, Mara and Alice drove south to the Little Rockies. The little white church where Mara meant to be married sat on a hill overlooking a ghost town. It came into sight before the dust settled around Alice's stopped car.

The bartender said reserving the church would be no problem. They didn't hold regular Sunday meetings anymore. "Might have to do some serious cleaning."

The bartender's words echoed as Mara rubbed a spot clear on the window. She peered in. Dust. Everywhere. Mara pictured the church filled with wild flowers. She would stand at the altar in an ivory dress with a lace jacket. Her hair would be braided, her feet brown and bare. Alice smiled at Mara as if she'd seen the very same thing.

Alice said that after her Bible study that night she would ask
Reverend Jones to officiate. Mara was in bed when Alice came
home and reading her book when Alice woke the next day.

Wind screamed through the screen windows. The cats did
figure eights around Mara's ankles.

"Well, what'd he say?"

Alice launched into a diatribe on Christians Mara couldn't
follow.

"He must have said no."

Alice nodded. "Said he couldn't do it, said you and Mac
had violated the sacraments of marriage. That you two had
openly lived together. He said he wouldn't be made a fool
of."

Mara sighed, picturing the reverend, his handlebar mustache and cowboy boots. She pictured him stamping his foot,
pointing his finger like a pistol.

It perplexed Alice that Mara wasn't disturbed by her news.
She went on, "Well, there are others, ministers. You can
always get the justice of the peace."

Mara smiled; the plump, middle-aged justice of the peace
was a divorcée. Encouraged by the smile, Alice suggested they
register at the Mercantile after lunch.

The clerk led mother and future daughter-in-law past racks of
shovels and rakes, galvanized tubs and plastic tubing, toward
"Domestics."

The plates were thin, flowered patterns, not the thick solid
stoneware Mara had always imagined she'd use for entertaining.
The clerk followed Mara, steno pad in hand, making a list of

items Mara hadn't acquired in living on her own or with Mac. The clerk tapped her pencil impatiently. None of the modern appliances, whipped cream pressurizers, appealed to Mara. The sales clerk thought she'd never seen a more listless bride.

Alice fingered yard goods in the Penney's store, wondering aloud about dresses for the bridesmaids. "Hunh?" Mara answered, then pretended to feel several sheer floral materials. She sleepwalked behind Alice, trying to conjure up a bridesmaid, as Mac's mother finished her errands.

At the bank, the plumber's, the drugstore, and the grocery, Alice introduced the reticent Mara only as her "daughter-in-law." Alice beamed, buying steak and wine. Mara purchased a *Bride's* magazine.

The wine, Mara knew, was a concession for company. Alice poured a pink chablis into empty shrimp cocktail glasses, while Mara licked a finger to turn another page of her magazine.

"Any ideas?" Alice asked. Mara shook her head and sipped her wine. Alice began tearing lettuce for salad. Mara turned page after page, pausing only to sip more wine. Her sense of chronology became comfortably confused. The two of them sat before empty, greasy plates before Mara remembered Alice even setting the meal on the table. "That was good."

Alice tipped her glass, waiting for the last slow drop of wine to roll into her mouth, then set the jar down announcing she had a headache. "I'm going to bed. Maybe you ought to go visit Alan."

Mara washed dishes. She heard Alice get out of bed and make her disoriented way down the hall. Mara turned to see Mac's mother wrapped in a sheet. "Maybe you ought to go visit Alan."

Mara wanted to read her book. Instead, she took Alice's keys, backing out the driveway into a blinding sunset.

Alan invited her into his trailer. He filled her in on the plot of a television show they continued to watch and offered Mara a beer. Alan curled at one end of the davenport in his work clothes. Mara sat at the other end, on the edge of one cushion. During a commercial, she commented on how clean his trailer was. Alan nodded.

"My cousin came to visit. Left the place in better shape than when she arrived."

Mara nodded, unable to think of a reply. Together, she and Alan sat on the davenport, not speaking, until the program ended, as if their careful boredom kept the place clean.

Mara began to make leaving motions. Alan stood and followed her out. He showed her the cantaloupe in his garden, grinning with smudged welder's pride. Dark had fallen around the screen throbbing in his living room.

Alice, in a white uniform, let the cat out as Mara pulled in the drive. Ten thirty, time Alice left for the hospital. She flipped off Johnny Carson. Mara handed Alice her keys. In a moment of understanding, she said, "Think I'll take the bus back to the big city tomorrow." She didn't say, "Here, neither of us can live as if we were alone."

Mara curled up on the sofa with her book. She heard what she thought was rain. She mistook the orphans crying on the doorstep for the coyote's howl. She told herself the cats ankling at eye level through Alice's unmown lawn were tigers.

. . .

"Why didn't you ever remarry?" Mara asked Alice to break the silence, as they drove the eighty miles to the bus stop next day. Alice yawned, "One husband's enough for any woman."

Mara asked, "How come?"

Miles later, Alice answered, "For instance, Forrest would have said you read too much. Once the children were born, he grumbled if I opened a book."

Mara thought about this as Alice's car advanced on a freight train, pulling parallel to the highway. At the stoplight in Havre, Alice asked, "Think we'll make it?"

Mara grinned, thinking of the little towns, the grain elevators, blips in the blurred landscape. "Yeah."

Alice hugged Mara and her eyes followed her to a seat. Each woman thought the other looked sad behind the tinted windows of the bus. Mara disappeared from Alice's sight long enough to dig a magazine of crosswords from her bag. She held it up for Alice to see. Mara had finished her book.

She slept clear into Great Falls. The sun was too warm, the landscape monotonous. She spent twenty minutes drinking coffee in the bus depot, listening to the pleas of a long-haired stranger, "Couldn't we go somewhere? Smoke a joint? Get a room?" Mara shook her head and heard herself begin to talk about abortions and babies and.

Toward the Continental Divide, the air cooled and the late afternoon sun threw trees and rocks into long shadowy relief. As the landscape disappeared into the dark, Sammy kept coming to mind. Mara saw that having a child might not be the last thing in the world.

Anniversary

To her co-workers, the new girl seemed too serious to have been a friend of Shelly's, the bookkeeper. They were only kidding the buyer's assistant about going home for lunch so faithfully; it was a way of making light of her infertility.

Mara paled in her basic black. She was both overdressed and underdressed in the air-conditioned office. She shivered at her desk, shuffling papers. The calendar, blank but for one appointment, read August 2. *White corners, venetian blinds. Egg yolks. Air-conditioned John Deere combines.* Three years to the date, the same glaring blue August day. Mara excused herself, joking that she'd be in the back office. The co-workers looked at one another. It wasn't funny, her trips to the ladies' room were so frequent.

There, Mara dabbed at her red-rimmed eyes as she stood before the mirror. Even she thought she looked like death warmed over. She shivered. The will of this little creature seemed immense and beyond Mara's control. It seemed to surround her like air; it was dangerous to breathe. It seemed to surround her like light; it was dangerous to look. Glumly, Mara regarded herself in the mirror. The blue, goose-bumped pallor of her skin turned a grayish pink there in the rest room's fluorescent light. Mara took a deep breath and flushed the toilet, should anyone see her come out of the back office. As its dull roar faded behind her, Mara returned to her desk.

She watched the clock. At ten minutes to four, she straightened her desk and announced she'd be leaving for the day. "I have a doctor's appointment."

Mara sat, waiting for Mac, on a concrete bench between the office building and the parking lot. The heat in the bench warmed her as she scanned the drive for Mac's van. The sun was so bright, she squinted. She lost track of time. When her co-workers began to filter out of the building, Mara looked at her wrist. She didn't wear a watch. Shelly called out, "Where's Mac?" Dazed, Mara shrugged her shoulders.

"Get in." Shelly helped her friend into her car. Mara should have been there half an hour ago. Shelly wove through rush-hour traffic toward the clinic. Breathlessly, the two women entered the doctor's office.

"I have an appointment with Dr. Smith."

Calmly, the receptionist asked the nature of Mara's visit, then informed Mara that Dr. Smith no longer performed that particular procedure. The red rim around Mara's eyes widened. "But I made an appointment."

"How far along are you?"

Mara guessed about twelve weeks.

Without another word, the nurse retreated into the doctor's examining rooms. Another woman within days of delivery stepped out of an examining room. Her smock no longer covered the elastic panel in her slacks. She wore dirty tennis shoes and Mara watched one arch flatten, before the nurse bustled back. "Dr. Frazier will see you."

Shelly sighed. She and Mara took seats in the waiting room, ignoring the magazines. A fern nodded near a vent. Shelly took Mara's hand, removed the ball of tissue from it. She listened as Mara quietly tried to vent her anger at the father of this, this growth. "You'd think he wanted me to have it," Mara hissed. Shelly nodded, but Mara could tell from her eyes that Shelly thought she sounded irrational.

"Miss Johnson?" The nurse smiled.

Shelly and Mara exchanged a look. Shelly squeezed Mara's hand. The expectant mothers in the waiting room wondered as Mara's sniffling subsided behind the door what this flat-bellied woman's problem could be.

The nurse, a tall, middle-aged brunette, took nervous looks at Mara. She read to herself from Mara's file, then said, "The doctor will be with you soon."

Mara studied the room, its dull green, the wood-grained Formica cabinets, the next Kleenex coming out of the box, the charts of female anatomy with the logo of drug companies in one corner. The door opened and a brisk, handsome man filled the room with currents of air. His dark curls were parted in an unsuccessful attempt to make them lie down. He wheeled a chair up to a small counter hung from the wall and began to ask questions, updating Mara's file.

Mara handed him the folded memo on Planned Parenthood paper, confirming her pregnancy, and began to cry. Abruptly, Dr. Frazier's scribbling pen stopped. A blob of blue ink collected on the tip.

"I'd like to talk about this first."

From the look that came over his face, Mara knew he wasn't

prepared to counsel her. "I made this appointment without a second thought. I'm engaged, the wedding's not until September, and we agreed we didn't want to start off this way. I didn't think. I didn't think the first time either, and months later, the bad dreams came."

The doctor nodded as though he knew which dreams Mara meant.

"You know what I realized just this afternoon? It is three years to the date this happened last." Mara shook, physically trying to shake the thought. "I asked myself if this was the purpose of my body? Of lovemaking? To abort each pregnancy? To take a pill each day?"

Frazier said nothing.

"What else can I do?"

The doctor mentioned adoption, then realized it wouldn't do. How could a young couple give up a child, even if it was born six short months after a wedding. And then, Mara realized Mac had no intention of marrying her. He'd harvested, combined, through the first terminated pregnancy. Afterward, he'd talked about the red-haired, barefoot tot in overalls they would someday have. But it was the wheat, the harvest, he was faithful to. He'd drop what he was doing every July, flooring, pounding nails, building granaries, felling trees, to go drive that combine in circles. This time he'd come back from the homestead early, muttering "Mary" or "marry" in his sleep. Yet, this time, he couldn't even drive her to the clinic. Mara blew her nose.

The doctor began a little story about a child born with a birth defect. The parents had known before she was born that she would likely have a handicap. They'd allowed the pregnancy to go full term. The girl, confined to a wheelchair, grew up to be a fine violinist. One day, the mother asked, "Aren't you glad we had you?" And the girl flatly said, "No."

In Mara's state of mind, she could not apply the doctor's story to her situation in any way. Was she supposed to see that children are not always grateful to be in the world? Mara tried to look the doctor in the eye, but her vision blurred. The doctor fidgeted with his pen. Mara fidgeted with her ragged Kleenex and caught her breath in near hiccups between sobs. She had no more to say or words for what she wanted to say.

Frazier ended the fifteen-minute session scribbling, "I will not perform this operation in the patient's present emotional state." He laid a tan, well-manicured hand on Mara's shoulder. "Get yourself some counseling."

The nurse wrote the number of a counselor at a women's abortion clinic on a slip of paper. "Didn't you see Dr. Campbell about birth control once?" Mara remembered the scene in the waiting room: tearing off her clothes, calling for her mother fifteen hundred miles away. The doctor had removed the IUD just minutes after he'd inserted it, saying, "You shouldn't be reacting this way."

"Dr. Campbell." Mara repeated the name. "How is he?"

"He died," the nurse said. "This office has all his old records."

The Women's Clinic

At the Rocky Mountain Women's Clinic, abortions were performed once a week, en masse. There, the operation was cheap,
but professional. It was legal. There, a woman had the support
of other women. Mara pictured twenty to thirty women, re-
clining on army cots, under stiff white sheets. In the space
between the cots, each held the other's hand, forming a human
chain round a large, institutional room.

So the lunch hour Mara went to be counseled there, she was
surprised that the waiting room was so small. Maybe it was
just full of old magazines. Maybe because the clinic office was
lost in the catacombs of this old building, with one frosted
window on the real world, the dim light just made it seem
small.

The door eased closed behind her. To Mara's left was a
counter and a window into a small office. Three or four women
in street clothes looked up, hushed in mid-conversation by
Mara's arrival.

"I'm Mara." She felt hot and sticky in her office clothes,

nylons, skirt, heels, and jacket. She dressed these days better than she felt. The suit was appropriate to the over-air-conditioned office she worked in, where the chill turned her skin blue.

"I'm Martha," a woman in purple, head to toe, replied. She broke away from the group of idle volunteers, inviting Mara into another small room off the office. All of them expected her.

Mara was surprised how friendly the brown eyes behind Martha's thick glasses were. As she followed Martha into the room, Mara noticed Martha's hair shone and flowed down her back. Mara had expected to be looked up and down.

Taking a seat in a vinyl tufted chair, Mara kicked off her heels and propped her feet on a hassock. She tried to estimate the thickness of the door between this room and the office, to determine if the other volunteer counselors, pressing an ear up against the door, would hear. Mara didn't know Martha. She'd called the clinic and simply asked for a counselor. She'd let Martha listen, but Mara's story wasn't for everyone. Besides that, Mara expected a fight. After all, this *was* an abortion clinic. Mara had called them precisely because she knew she needed to be talked into it.

Martha sat diagonally across the cramped room from Mara in a canvas director's chair. Mara's own chair was the closest thing to the chaise longue she'd seen in psychiatrist cartoons she'd ever sat in. Martha handed Mara a Kleenex. Mara removed her glasses. Minutes passed in which neither woman said a word. Mara commented how comfortable she felt. Martha nodded.

The silence embarrassed Mara. Though the only clock in the room was strapped to Martha's wrist, Mara had the sense of time ticking by. She was not accustomed to speaking without being questioned. She took a deep breath and described her visit to Dr. Frazier.

Fat tears rolled down Mara's face and she wiped them away. "He said he wouldn't do it, unless I was counseled first. Here I am."

Martha made no reply.

"I don't know what happened that day. Mac missed his connection with me. He was supposed to drive me to the clinic. Shelly took me." Mara realized Martha couldn't know who these names referred to, but she continued, "Shelly and I, we've both been through this before. I knew what to expect: a night's aching around a laminaria. I don't know why I fell apart."

Mara waited for the counselor to tell her. Martha made no reply. Mara sniffed.

"I told Mac what happened. I laid into him for being late. That was unusual. He's never seen me so mad about such a little thing. A ride. We never argue because he won't argue back. He just clams up, like I'm always right, like I'm attacking him, like there is no argument. Like he is an asshole. That's how he responded at first and then, I turned my anger into pleading. I said, 'Let's have this child?' He didn't say anything. We were drinking Scotch and ice. I remember that. It was late afternoon and the sun deflected off our drinks, colored everything more yellow. I felt warm. I felt there could be a solution to this. I swallowed my anger, the ice melted. He listened to me. I thought we were working things out, little by little. But he still couldn't see a way to keep it. Thought it was all my fault, the pregnancy, that I tried to trap him. That I hadn't used birth control. We've been engaged all summer. I didn't see any need to trap him. I was as surprised as he was that I was pregnant. He's been gone so much all summer, we haven't made that much love. No way, he said, we couldn't keep it. The more I talked, the more he grinned sweetly, letting me talk. The ice jangled in his glass. He said he knew he'd slighted me this summer, being away so much. My problem is that I like solitude. I made up to him when he was home, so he'd keep leaving me alone. He cajoled me, said he'd make the time up to me, if I'd get an abortion. He threatened me, he wouldn't marry me if I kept it. I smiled; I didn't think he'd ever planned to marry me. The main reason we couldn't keep it, he said, was because he'd just changed jobs. We weren't well enough established. I've been looking for a job all summer."

Mara paused. She was gathering force. She was surprised at the sound of her own voice. She was not accustomed to being listened to.

"I tried to reason with him. I said it didn't matter how much money a person had, money had nothing to do with kids. You just find a way. I didn't know for certain if that was true. I just thought of it as I talked to him. It'd be a big chance to take, but he wasn't convinced. Thin ice.

"I said, 'Remember the first time. Every time a woman on a soap opera had a baby, I'd cry. You'd hug me and say, "Someday we'll have one too." I believed you. We've known each other five years. Isn't that long enough to know whether we're ready to take a risk?' He didn't say anything. We talked for a long time. We had a barbecue to go to. I made a salad, cubes of cantaloupe and watermelon and honeydew. Dangerous wielding that knife. Kept sniffing, trying to suck the tears back in. I was a composed drunk, after an hour or so. We went to the party. Neither of us said much to anyone that night. Mac didn't talk to me. The others told dirty jokes until it just became too chilly on the patio to go on.

"I've had one abortion. He didn't see me through that one. He was harvesting, he does every year for his uncle. Sometime between the end of July, the beginning of August. He had an excuse that time. It wasn't the way I wanted it. I wanted him to hold my hand. I went to see him on my way to Missoula, drove right up to his combine in the field. He stopped his circling for a couple minutes. Hugged me, said it was gonna be okay. That was before his uncle's second seizure, before Mary Lou started feeding her father applesauce. He met my bus on the return trip. I remember he bought me supper. I remember the drive on into Malta, I cuddled up to him just like I tried to do that afternoon of the barbecue. I kept telling *him* it was gonna be okay. He didn't say much. The gun rack rattled behind us in the pickup. He held me tight that night. I felt like a kid. I was a kid."

Mara blew her nose. Martha didn't move.

"Bothers me now, he didn't go through it with me that first time. I said I'd do it this time, but he was gonna have to help me through it. I put it off until after harvest so he could. Must be the thirteenth, fourteenth week now. Late. Then he couldn't even give me a ride to the doctor's for a laminaria insert. That's not even an abortion. All he had to do was sit in the waiting room, fifteen minutes. That was his mistake. I could have gone through with it, but he was late.

"He doesn't know what it's like. This time I wanted him right there in the cubicle with me. I wanted him to hold my hand, to watch them. I wanted him to see the little knot gag the machine. He won't even make love to me; he's afraid he'll knock up against that little knot. His very own knot. He likes the way my breasts are, though.

"I called my mother the night after I talked to him. I told her I was pregnant. I told her about the first abortion. I told her about the summer's worth of problems with him. I'd glossed the problems over in my letters home. They were full of descriptions, scenery and weather. She heard me out, but she thinks I ought to talk to a counselor too. My idea that it's ethically, if not psychologically, unsound to have more than one abortion sounded crazy to her, who never had a choice. She thinks I'm off my rocker to think I can re-create the first fetus by letting this one grow. That alarms her. She just wants the best for me. She wanted Mac to bring me right home.

"I haven't worked all summer. I have no money. I couldn't afford to go home. I said, who's gonna hire a pregnant woman if I pack up and leave this job I just got, if I come home again. She didn't answer. She said, talk to a counselor. Do what I thought best.

"I'm not thinking very straight these days. All my girl friends abort their pregnancies. They have better things to do. They think I'm crazy. The doctor thinks I'm crazy. It seems crazy. But it isn't the purpose of my body to make love and then abort every time I get pregnant, is it?

"The first time, I was just like my girl friends. No way, I thought, I could support a child. We were living hand to mouth, but having fun. When I left him after the first abortion, I was tired of drinking and taking drugs and sleeping with his buddies. We weren't getting anywhere, just older. We're all so selfish nowadays."

Martha cleared her throat. The hands on her watch dial read a quarter to one.

"I know I'm not making much sense. You've listened to me for an hour. When will you tell me what to do?"

"Well, you *can* have repeated abortions without physiological damage. We're set up here to—"

"But, do you think I'd get pregnant twice like this if I really wanted an abortion? And one, exactly three years after the date of the first?"

"That often happens to women who've had previous abortions."

"Well, what do *you* make of that? It seems to me like this kid wants to be born, like its will is greater than mine."

Martha shrugged.

"Do you have children of your own?"

Martha shook her head. "I've had an abortion. My ex-husband was a student then. You know one thing we women tend to forget? Even the men who will hold your hand through the operation can't know what it's like. We have to understand that and be careful how we react. Don't destroy a relationship you value just because the fetus didn't come out of his body."

"I don't seem to have much of a relationship."

"Some people will say you're selfish to keep the child, that you're only thinking of yourself and not the baby's future, when you have a child and no husband. Think of the problems. Try to imagine what it's like to sit home Friday and Saturday because you don't have the money for a baby-sitter or you can't find one. Try to picture yourself carrying a diaper bag with you everywhere you go. Try to imagine listening to stories of what your single friends do, the fun they have. Add up the costs of child care and formula and clothing and medical expenses. Of course, there are social programs to help single mothers out."

Mara didn't hear Martha. Martha's watch read five of one. Mara began collecting herself to go, without looking at the counselor. She said, "That baby won't know how poor I am.

That was Mac's problem. He thinks he has to give a child the best money can buy. It's an excuse. We're all making excuses. We think we know what's best. It's nothing but a thick cover for our fear." Mara stood.

Martha sighed.

Dance with the Moon

Mara had thought riviera blinds would be better than curtains in their new apartment, but two uncertain months had passed and nothing but the drapery rods hung at the windows. In the meantime, Mara had decided she liked the windows just the way they were, and since it was a second-floor apartment she left them uncovered. Looking out, she could see the boughs of a tall, dancing pine, the glare of streetlights, power lines, and sometimes stars. Looking in, a voyeur would see a double bed centered in a sterile white room, an antique dresser pushed up against one sand-blasted plasterboard wall.

Yes, Mara liked the neat corners of the window and likened the view to a painting. Tonight, as she tried to sleep, moonlight fell across the crumpled sheets. She seemed able to feel the light and opened her eyes. She saw back through all the years to similar restless nights as a child. Then, she had tossed and turned in her old double bed, beside her sleeping sister.

Tonight, she lay still until her eyes adjusted to the shapes in the room. She filled clothing hung in the closet with figures.

She stared at the floorboards until the dark room was illuminated. She studied the angle the bedroom door made with the wall and the dark beyond the angle. The tiniest sound magnified itself, she looked so intensely at that door. She expected a familiar form, even more solid than the dark, to appear there. The burglar with a key. She expected Mac.

When the form failed to appear and the sheet of light began to slip from the bed, Mara sank a fist into the pillow beside her own. A dull, muffled sound. Taking the fist back to herself, Mara noticed the graceful arc of an arm. She punched the pillow again and the arm reappeared. Alarmed, she sat up in bed, as did the shadow the arms were a part of. Experimentally, Mara hugged herself, and the arms disappeared.

She took a deep breath and watched her breasts swell in shadow. The breasts of both women swelled. Mara threw herself on the shadow, panting, and it disappeared. But as the sound of her breath and her heartbeat grew loud in her ears, Mara pushed away from the mattress. The torso of the other woman played on the wall with Mara's same swollen breasts, taut belly, and long legs. Mara reached for her and the shadow's arm lifted out of reach. Indignant, Mara put one fist on her hip and the other woman mimicked her with an unintended flounce of hair. Seeing that this other woman was playful, Mara arched her back provocatively and fell back on the bed. The figure rushed into Mara's arms.

The pair played this way until the soft night jerked like a muscle around them. Exhausted, they fell asleep. When Mara woke, her lover was gone. She felt no grief; instead, she understood her distaste for curtains. She no longer had anything to hide.

Cheerios

"I've decided to have the baby."

Mac looked up from behind his cereal box. Milk dripped from his spoon. "Do you have any idea what you're saying?"

Mara nodded.

"Do you have any idea what an immense responsibility you're taking on?"

Mara nodded again.

"You're crazy." Then, as Mac drank the milk from his bowl, Mara heard his ride pull up outside. Silently, Mac gathered his jacket, hat, and gloves. Mara padded around after him, barefoot, trying to give him the usual parting kiss. So far as she was concerned nothing had changed, having a child was a passive act. Mac ignored her. He slammed the door on the dim gray morning more firmly than usual, saying, "I'll see you later."

. . .

Mac did not come home for supper. He wasn't at Lane's shop or at happy hour. Mara called Shelly and said, "I feel like dancing." She dressed, proud of the flat-bellied effect and the spark in her eye. She ran no risk of running into Mac at the Baghdad. Her only partners there would be black men and gays. When Mara pulled up out front, Shelly stood in a crowd on the sidewalk, waiting to have her ID checked. Mara laughed; both women were far beyond eighteen. In her heels, Mara stood nearly as tall as her friend. Cars honked at them. Men standing in line winked harmlessly.

They could hear the beat of Donna Summer's "Last Dance" waft out past the bouncer, through the door. The heat of dancers already crammed on the dance floor gave Mara the impression of entering a heart where flashing lights and throbbing music and writhing bodies were indistinguishable from one another. She and Shelly fought the crowd for a table, but before the waitress could bring drinks, a mouthful of teeth requested this dance.

Mara could feel the knot in her belly rock from side to side and she held her belly in both palms proudly. She explained to her partners, during lulls in the music's fast pace, taking whiffs of the scent sweat made with their clothing, that she was going to be a momma soon. As the word spread, others, until now shadows leaning against the wall, asked for a turn. Mara forgot her drink.

At two, her long hair stuck to her face in damp, thick lines, and Mara declined breakfast, hoping Mac would be home waiting. She drove across town, likening the traffic lights to the disco, a simple matter of letting one's focus go. Stopped at a red light, she felt a surge of moisture in her tight jeans.

·   ·   ·

Blood. Mara saw it by the harsh bathroom light. It looked like smoke dripping into the cool water. "Damn."

She cursed the familiar snore coming from the bedroom. She undressed, wearing only a fresh pair of panties to bed. It proved to be a restless night, as the bleeding gathered force. Mara propped herself up in bed beside the baby's father, hoping the angle of her body would stop the flow. She changed pair after pair of panties and sat on a towel. She did everything she could to keep from staining Mac's side of the bed.

Mara was on the telephone when Mac woke. He heard her ask, "What can I do about the bleeding?"

She propped up her feet for the rest of the day, reading *Birth Without Fear*. Mac ran the vacuum. Mara napped. Mac lifted the book from the arm of her chair. He read, "During pregnancy, women can maintain their usual level of activity."

Mac cooked her bacon and eggs, brewed fresh ground coffee, just as he had in their first sweet and sleepy days. Mara wondered at this mixed message as she listened to soft piano jazz on his stereo. They shared a joint and she ceased to wonder.

Monday, Mara laughed once at work and Mac fell asleep in front of the television. At 4:30 a.m. Wednesday morning, Mara urged him out of the flickering blue light to bed. The next evening he carried in sacks of groceries, while Mara ate dinner with a friend. The friend had two little boys. Brian, the younger, insisted that Mara kiss him. Without her kiss, he explained, he wouldn't be able to sleep.

Mac left for the weekend. Mara did the Sunday crossword. Monday night, the incessant barking of a dog woke them. And the next day, it rained.

Mara and Shelly looked at an apartment in a swinging singles complex. The next day, Shelly decided to give Lane a second chance. That weekend, Mara went to Spokane. She watched her hostess's cat move in the sunlight. The hostess was a single mother. Mara returned to find blood oozing from stitches over Mac's left eye. He'd been in a barroom brawl the night before.

Monday, Shelly found an incriminating letter to Lane in the trash. Mara changed the dressing over Mac's eye. The next morning, she came back to bed after she'd dressed for work. She floated to the rhythm of Mac's sleeping breath: he knows no more about being a man than I know about being a woman, neither of us quite knows how to be human. At midweek, Mara convinced Shelly to rent the apartment, giving her friend a stern feminist lecture. They put down a deposit. Mac brought a friend home for Thursday supper. While Mara washed the dishes, the men planned their weekend.

Mac bought the Harley in Great Falls, while Mara began to read a book she'd read before. Sunday, she packed her books, her rocker, and most of the kitchen utensils. Shelly carried the boxes down the steps to a borrowed truck and back up the steps to their new apartment. She explained, "You're pregnant and should do no lifting."

Mac blinked his black eye in surprise when he returned to find Mara gone. She'd left him a pepper shaker and a dirty ashtray. He lay in bed, staring at the glitter in the ceiling, wanting to curl into the fetal position he'd used when his father died, used the time she'd left before. All the time he lay there, Mac thought how equitable and ordinary the past month had been.

Monday, Mara thought about giving the baby up for adoption and Shelly in a moment of paralysis called Mac to ask if leaving Lane had been the right thing. Feeling a flicker of sexual interest in her boss, Mara felt better the next day. She kept her first prenatal appointment with Dr. Frazier. By the end of the week, she decided she liked the motel-like sterility of the swinging singles apartment.

Friday, Mac's landlord called Mara. In excited Greek, he explained he'd gone to collect the rent, disturbing some sort of stag party. Apparently, Rick, Lane, and Jack sat all around the edge of the double bed where Mac lay, shooting a pistol into the ceiling. Mara assured Mr. Stergios the rifles lined up at the door were nothing more than Mac's efforts to move. Nothing to call the police about. The landlord's excited accent subsided into English. Mara hung up and smiled.

Self-Sufficiency

Mara's shoes were lined up heel to heel in her closet. Her bed, the one Shelly grew up in, was made without a wrinkle. Shelly was out. That was the message Mara gave callers, as she sat at the kitchen table reading.

Their new kitchen was a bright peach color, a strained coordination with the living room carpet. They were short of cupboard space and Shelly's Tupperware sat out, like other women display antique dishes and friendship cups. She'd spread a crocheted tablecloth across their Formica dinette set. Mara's mug left a brown ring on the cloth. She was careful to set the mug in the same brown ring, sip after sip.

"I was glad she was masturbating," Mara read. "That way I would not have to spend hours making her barrel weep, locating the minuscule escarpment inside her that required incessant stimulation. But would her motions be an invitation or a warding me off with her own self-sufficiency?"

Mara closed the book; "or a warding me off with her own self-sufficiency"? Self-sufficiency? Mara closed her eyes. She opened them, then rose from her chair. Slipped into a heavy sweater and out the door, walking east on South Avenue past the grocery, the car lot. It was midnight, Sunday, and neon lights cast a dramatic glow on the street. Patrol cars cruised slowly past her. There was little traffic.

Crazy. She couldn't be sure he'd be home or alone. "Self-sufficiency"? But it was imperative to admit her vulnerability, her need.

Halfway across town, Mara stood at an empty intersection waiting for the light to change. The same patrol cars passed her, more curious this time, amazed by the distance she'd covered on foot. They seemed to ask, "Don't you recognize the danger?" Then, as if reading her thoughts, they passed on. "I'm a big girl, bent on a mission. If I walk briskly and unafraid, no one will touch me."

After eighteen blocks, the concrete and neon signs began to give way to landscaped lawns. Trees materialized out of the darkness at regular intervals, as though some thought had been put into their locations. With this change of scene, Mara herself was amazed her resolve didn't waver. Her legs tired, but her feet skipped up the steps to Mac's apartment.

The door was unlocked. Inside, moonlight shone through curtainless windows. There was a curious light to the close, heavy air. The place smelled of sleep.

Mara let herself in, familiarly. She stood in the doorway of the bedroom for a moment, studying the configurations of the sheets. A figure filled one half of the bed. It stirred as Mara's weight depressed the mattress.

"Hi."

"Hello."

"What are you doing here?"

"I have something to say." But Mara felt an urgent need to pee. The need ruined the cinematic way she'd envisioned the scene as she'd crossed town. Both listened to the loud sound of her urine into the toilet, listened to it ruin the momentum of what she'd had to say.

"I need you."

The figure made no reply.

"I wish we could let down our defenses. Quit pretending we're self-sufficient."

Still, there was no reply.

"Couldn't we just admit . . . we need each other?" Mara leaned over and put her arms around him. She laid her head on his shoulder.

He spoke. She could feel his throat vibrate. "You're having second thoughts, aren't you?"

"Not at all."

Mara sat up, incredulous that he'd misunderstand when she'd spoken so plainly. "I'm a strong woman. I want this baby. I can fix my own breakfast and you can fix yours, but we need each other." Mara heard his clock tick. "That's all I have to say."

She blew her nose. It was another unlikely sound. She bent to hug Mac again, smelling the sour odor of his sleep. He wanted only to sleep. Then, sniffling, she left the room.

"You're welcome to stay," Mac hollered after her. Mara shook her head. "I'll give you a lift on my way to work, around five."

Mara shook her head and closed Mac's door securely behind her.

·   ·   ·

Stepping with her right foot, Mara doubted she'd trembled enough in his arms. Stepping with her left, she wondered why he hadn't been more alarmed by her strange presence in the apartment. She'd meant to enter like an intruder. He did not follow her. Patrol cars did. All the way home.

The Log and the Leg

The first time Mac hurt his knee, he'd been a kid. Just out of high school. Just after his dad died, he spent his inheritance on a Corvette. He ditched it after a month, a mile south of town.

The knee bothered him some, but then all flooring contractors complained about their knees. When he and Mara had started over, he'd decided to change careers. He switched to sawing trees. In fact, the day she skipped her appointment for the abortion, she'd ridden up to Nine Mile with him and watched the trees fall. She'd worn a hard hat and served a picnic lunch on a stump. She said nothing about the whine of chain saws, less about the thunderous sound a ponderosa made. She liked the smell of pine and sawdust.

He remembered all that when he came out of anesthesia a month later. The sharp antiseptic smell of his room on the orthopedic ward reminded him of his mother, the nurse. A thick white cast immobilized his right leg. He could vaguely remember Lane, Rick, the guys gathered around his bed the night before. They'd left a six-pack, a can of snoose, and a magazine, though he hadn't been able to focus their faces through his drugged eyes. He remembered nothing of his hours in the operating room, little of the time spent X-raying the knee.

When the log came rolling down off the hill, he'd been leaning against a Cat. It was coffee break and he'd been telling the operator what a fine woman she was, but not for him. Neither of them saw it coming. The runaway log pinned his leg up against the machine. By the time the guys could move it, the log had crushed the knee joint. They loaded him in a pickup and wound down out of the hills. With each bump, he knew how useless that leg would be. And once the truck pulled out on the highway, tears oozed out from under his eyelids.

"How do you feel?"

Mac studied the sky outside his third-floor window, through the venetian blinds. He looked at the clock up on the wall, nine thirty, before he turned to the voice.

"Feeling no pain." Mac grinned through his disheveled hair. Mara saw the old flash in his eyes. "How about you?"

A thick-waisted nurse bustled into the room. She took the patient's vitals and closed his magazine, *Playboy*. "The doctor will be in to see you soon."

Mara stood at the end of the bed, shyly holding the big toe that stuck out the end of the cast. "This is the first you'll have talked to him since the operation?"

Mac nodded to Mara's question as the doctor strode into the room. Mara sat down in the corner, uncertain whether to remove her coat. This would be the first time he'd seen her blossoming body. She decided one crisis was enough. In her lap, she held a book. She didn't know who the doctor took her for.

"Well, you banged your knee up pretty good, though you'll regain partial use of it with some therapy. Probably won't ever run again."

Mac's face betrayed nothing. Mac took the news mutely. It occurred to him that he'd never be able to lay another kitchen floor or limb a tree. Workmen's compensation. Occupational therapy.

Mara misread his silence. She thought of the added injury, of having no income at the same time all kinds of medical bills piled up. She half-gloated, thinking months of immobility might change his mind about fatherhood. The idea was so lovely to her, she even entertained notions of offering to come back, nurse him back to health, help him with the expense. Her blouse shifted over her belly and her reverie broke in time to hear the doctor say, "I've prescribed a painkiller for you. Ring the nurse's station when you need it."

An awkward silence filled the room once the doctor left. Neither Mara nor Mac knew what to offer the other. They heard the clock tick. Both stared out the window. The clouds drifted to the sound of traffic below. Looking down across Broadway, Mara could see the ob/gyn clinic across the street. She turned away and said, "I brought you a book."

When they'd lived together, she'd encouraged him to read. A man who, unlike her father, did not think and reflect was a mystery to Mara. Mac seemed to like regional history best, the journals of Lewis and Clark, biographies of trappers and mountain men.

Handing him the book, Mara explained, "Novellas, three long short stories in one volume. Macho romances. One's about the son of a rancher who takes revenge . . ."

Mac's thick fingers thumbed the pages of Mara's book. He thanked her, though he knew he wouldn't read it. Mara toyed with the buttons on her coat still wondering if she should stay or go. Her down jacket was too warm. "Is there anything I can get you?" She hoped he'd ask her back.

"That can of snoose."

Disappointed, she crossed the room carrying the Skoal. A plug of tobacco would make his kiss matter-of-fact. If they were going to connect, the moment would have to be now. And Mara knew she would have to initiate. She held the can behind her back and, tentatively, leaned over.

Caught off guard, Mac failed to turn his head. Mara's kiss landed on one unshaven cheek. She stepped back, perhaps too soon. He caught her cheek in his rough hand and held her face for a moment. It was a gesture he'd never made before.

Mara heard Mac tap the lid of the snoose box once and turned at the door to say her practiced line, "Well, the baby's legs are strong." She patted her belly and disappeared.

The long walls of the orthopedic ward leaned in on her as she made her way to the elevator. She pushed the button for street level and descended. She pitied the poor man for his paralysis.

An Old Wives' Tale

A full moon and a streetlight shone on the old snow. It was silver outside the room. A how-to book rested spine up on the table beside her bed. The digits on the clock were blue at 1:15. Mara wrestled with the pillow and the covers and settled into a half curl on her right side. She was just beginning to dream, when she wet the bed.

Mara soaked her nightgown, a long wallpaper-print flannel. Wearily, rising to change, Mara continued to pour out of herself. She watched the edges of the puddle on the floor creep away from her feet. Stupefied, she bent to look between her legs.

Across the hall, her roommate settled into a drunken sleep. Mara knocked on her door a third time. "Shelly?" Mara said. "It's coming. The time is come. We better go. Shelly?"

Shelly warmed the car as Mara changed pair after pair of soaking underwear. At last in dark slacks and an old flannel shirt, Mara picked her way across an icy parking lot. The car idled in a cloud of exhaust. The wind chafed Mara's legs.

Shelly asked where Mara's suitcase was.

"On the top shelf of my closet."

Shelly, impatient, "Did you remember your toothbrush?"

Mara shook her head. Shelly saw Mara's hands shake also and her teeth chatter. She made Mara buckle her seat belt and backed the car out without further questioning.

Mara remembered her confident hands turning the steering wheel toward "Emergency." "Emergency" was locked. A sleepy janitor answered Mara's insistent knock. A woman all in white handed Mara a square of cloth, covered with a print like her father's old shirts. Another white woman in quiet shoes pushed a chair on wheels into the back side of Mara's knees and she sat. Swiftly, Mara rode down over the dull gleam of fluorescent lights on highly waxed tiles.

Pull a string on the square of cloth and two armholes unfold. The woman in quiet shoes and Shelly helped Mara into a gown and another bed. This bed was higher and narrower than the one at home, the sheets more crisp.

Mara studied the room by light from the hallway. An overstuffed chair. A clock at two. A sink hung from the wall. There were no windows in the room.

Quiet Shoes returned, wheeling an electronic device. She attached a belt with an electrode to Mara's waist and the device. Tiny nervous digits appeared in red on its screen. Paper, the width of toilet tissue, churned out of the machine. Quiet Shoes left the room. Mara rose on her elbows and looked at the device. Underneath the digits, the screen was labeled HEARTBEAT.

Mara was fascinated. The numbers changed quickly as butterflies beat their wings. A third white woman came into the room and snapped a rubber glove efficiently over her hand. She covered two fingers with a substance out of a thick tube.

Politely, she asked Mara to part her legs. She ran two fingers up inside of her and claimed to feel nothing.

Yet another white woman came, snapping a rubber glove over her hand, and covered her fingers with more jelly. She ran her fingers up inside of Mara. Mara could feel her fist. Looking down between her knees, Mara could see an arm from the elbow up. The white woman was satisfied. She thought she felt a face.

Every hour on the hour, a white woman came snapping her rubber glove and feeling around inside of Mara. Mara was hypnotized by the pulse rate flashed on the screen, the printout curling up on the floor. Shelly tried to sleep in the uncomfortable overstuffed chair. Mara's belly rose like a mountain and fell like a wave. The clock ticked toward 7 a.m.

The number flashing on the screen divided in half. The needle on the dial swung crazily to the right in response to Mara's scream. She felt no pain, but there were fewer heartbeats than before. A rubber glove came running and explained the problem was an electrical short in the machine. She patted Mara's hand. She asked if Mara wanted something to drink. Mara ordered milk.

At 8 a.m., a white woman Mara had never seen before flashed her diamond ring in the dark room. The ring was beautiful. She asked Mara's name and adjusted the uncomfortable electrode in the belt. Shelly snored. Diamond Ring sent another white woman into the room to tell all about her ski trip. Ski Trip had her hair done up in braids. Mara liked her. She had clean, capable hands. She was not white, but green. In the distance, a woman moaned. Mara drifted in and out of sleep. A dull ache at the base of her spine woke her.

Mara shifted in the bed. Even Shelly was green now, with

blue puffs over her shoes. She spoke through a mask. Mara moaned. Shelly put a cool cloth on Mara's forehead.

Mara dreamed of going to the bathroom. Green disconnected the belt. Mara sat on the chilly fixture in the closet of her room. There were silver rails to either side. Mara climbed back into bed, Daddy's print falling away from her backside. On her back, Mara's hairy legs fell apart. A reassuring man patted her crotch. He suggested an internal monitor.

Mara moaned no. A green woman crossed the room with a flimsy white stick, a sharp spring on one end. Green said the stick was for safety's sake: "Would you like a sedative?" Mara shook her head. It distressed Mara that she couldn't relieve herself of this pressure, even in a bathroom. She looked around for someone to blame. Men paced the hallway, cigars in their pockets. Mara rolled over on her side, the monitor stuck out of her behind like a tail.

The words "I want to push" pushed out Mara's mouth. Greens bustled at the foot of the bed. Mara could have shit in their faces. Shelly advised her to pant. Mara did and the pressure went away.

And returned as greens wheeled Mara's bed through the double doors across the hall.

This new room was mostly dark and shiny. Everything in it gleamed. An intense overhead lamp bore down on a table, long as a body. Someone dragged a cloth over the table and positioned a chair at one end.

Ski Trip asked Mara to lie on the table. Mara tried, though the wheeled bed she was on seemed to want to push away. Mara might fall between the two platforms onto the floor. The pressure returned and passed without panting. A voice sug-

gested Mara put her feet in the stirrups. She did, noticing the
dirty socks she'd worn ever since she'd closed the how-to book
and first tried to sleep. She noticed the long dark hairs on her
pale legs. She noticed the cross wires in the door's window
and a strange man's face staring through it. She noticed the
angle of the lamp, glamorous and hot on her huge labia. A
voice, with her back to Mara, arranged a blanket in a glass
box. A man with glasses, nose pressed flat by a mask, washed
his hands in one corner of the room. Shelly's admonitions to
pant grew distant as Mara gathered up her insides and turned
inside out.

The cervix eased over the skull.

Shelly said, "It's . . ." she said . . . "a girl."

A tiny body lay in a puddle of blood on the table. It blinked
at the chrome, the bright lights. It gasped and captured a
breath. The air shrank in the room.

Someone handed it to Mara, laid the tiny body in her armpit.
A rope of flesh trailed between them across Mara's belly. Body
and Mara blinked at one another. How old she looked. How
slick she was. How misshapen the skull.

According to the book, she was supposed to suck from Mara
now. This was the thirty-fifth week of gestation, that point
in its development, medical science believed, when a fetus
developed its sucking instinct. She took one look at the size
of Mara's breast and turned away. It was twice the size of her
tiny head.

Ski Trip wheeled her away in the glass box, bound in a
blanket.

The man in glasses threaded a needle and chatted and sewed
Mara up.

Mara told the man she'd like to fart in his face.

Shelly passed out.

The muscles in Mara's legs twitched uncontrollably. Her uterus contracted.

She had Jell-O with whipped cream for lunch.

She flew up and down the maternity ward for hours, unable to sleep.

She took sitz baths.

She did not urinate or move her bowels for a week.

She pumped her breasts.

She asked the man in glasses about the old wives' tale. He nodded his head. "Atmospheric pressure," that's what he called the moon and the waves. Indeed, the majority of births in any given month occur on a full moon. There is statistical proof.

In fact, Mara sat in her rocker and did not sleep for a year. She stared out the window and listened for her breath. Beyond the glass, light preyed on the mountainside as two hands. The moon rose out of a form darker than the dark.

Baby's Breath

The humidifier hissed and the television spoke and through the door, Mara could not hear her breathe. Sometimes, Mara was able to forget the tiny body curled up under its quilt, behind the bars of its bed. She was able to read or write a letter or putter around the kitchen. Or talk on the telephone.

But every so often, the baby whimpered and wrestling with the quilt, turned over. Sometimes, she would roll up against the bars of the crib, and the furniture would speak. Mara was so afraid the sound would wake her, she held her breath too. Mara listened for the whimper to develop into a cry. Mara was there if it did, to pace the small area between their beds or to plug the cry with a breast. Mara was there, but she hoped the baby wouldn't wake. Mara needed time too.

But sometimes, minutes would go by after a whimper and the silence grew. There were voices on the television or a character who spoke in a book. Or the sound of Mara's pencil traveling across the page as she carried on a dialogue with a friend thousands of miles away. And the silence grew. If too many minutes passed without a whimper, that made Mara nervous too. Mara turned the knob slowly and tiptoed to her bedside. Mara stood very still and listened. Sometimes, there wasn't any sound. Sometimes, the breathing was too shallow to hear.

Mara would bend over the railing and place a hand on the small of her back. Sometimes, she could detect no rise or fall. Mara held her breath, and when five seconds passed without motion, she would give the baby a shove and the baby would give Mara a histrionic sigh. The baby took a weary breath of the dark, moist air.

Sometimes, Mara thought she detected a rising and falling, but she always had to double-check; her heartbeat made her hand tremble slightly as the ribs around her daughter's lungs moved under the skin.

Sometimes, the baby would roll over, wide-eyed, and after a long look, blink, taking the looming face of her mother into her head.

Some nights, it was so bad Mara would check every fifteen minutes. Mara would go to bed herself and stare out the window and keep listening. She counted the seconds between breaths, watching the rise and fall of the baby's ribs. Some nights, Mara threw back the covers and jostled the baby until she could hear her. Mara felt so responsible for her breathing, she couldn't sleep herself. The only tragedy Mara could imagine was the baby's silently turning blue as Mara slept in the dark.

A Letter to Mother

Momma,

How long has it been since I've called you by that name?
In the seventh grade once, I called you Momma and the
kids laughed. To keep the kids from laughing, I shortened
"Momma" to "Mom," though the word felt strange in my
mouth. Now in grad school, I run across this line in a
textbook: "the mere cry of 'mama' has in it a soothing
element; insofar as it is the continuation of the act of
sucking, it produces a kind of hallucinatory satisfaction."
Momma, you're with me. You're with me, sure as I pat the
place beside me on the step.

Tomorrow, you'll call me, dutifully saying my name,
tentatively as I call my own daughter "Alison." I remember
you used to call home every day after school, from the
office, to assign kitchen chores and wonder what came in
the mail. When there was a letter among Dad's professional
literature and the bills, you'd have me open it and read.

Grandma's letters would go on and on about the weather, how her garden grew. How patient you seemed as I stumbled over her handwriting and how impatient I was to come to the end of her aches and pains. The two of you wrote each other in sentences that dropped the "I." Always wondered why.

I keep a list beside the telephone of things I can tell you, things that will give you an impression of well-being, keep you from worrying. Raspberries. A friend has a patch of them in his backyard. Though times are bad, the raspberries thrive. They are so ripe, they fall off in my hand. Like jewels, there is always one more red and plump than the last. I fill my pail in no time. The branches prick my arms and the leaves flutter into Alison's fascinated face.

My mouth waters for your homegrown tomatoes and I'd like to have a garden myself. My neighbors grow tomatoes in tubs. I tried that, but mine turned yellow and wilted when the volcano erupted. A natural disaster. When I whispered we were quarantined because it was snowing sand, Alison smiled for the first time. There's a move among the family housing tenants to organize a community garden. The university is considering a plot next to the golf course. So, if all goes well, I should have tomatoes of my own late next August. A full five weeks after yours ripen. I'll have zucchini to give away. My friends have been generous with their garden surplus, but it's not the same as getting my own hands dirty.

Do you realize Alison will be eight months old this Sunday? It does not seem possible. Yet, she's twice what she weighed at birth. Grows like a weed. After all my long hours of rocking the colic away, Dr. Carter has

supplemented breast milk with soybean formula. I'm
convinced cow's milk is too rich for the human system. And
I have started her on cereal, though I'm having to pry her
mouth open with the spoon. The breast pumping on my
coffee breaks was getting old. I'd sit in that cubicle,
pumping away, pouring the precious ounces in a jar I held
between my knees. One day, after three ounces, the jar
slipped and spilled. The white fluid ran toward the drain in
the next cubicle. Can you imagine what that woman must
have thought?

And that rocker I bought at the estate sale we went to?
The seat was cracked when I bought it, but a week ago it
split clear across. Pinched my bottom! Before I could have
it repaired, we had another fit of colic. Just as Alison
calmed down, stroking my breast while I sang "Rockabye
My Baby," the cross supports loosened and the chair
dumped us both on the floor. I threw the pieces away.

Momma, when I was born could you still remember
being a little girl? I can. I remember your moments of
anger, when you threatened, "Just wait until you have
children of your own." (I have yet to pass this curse along.)
I can imagine the way you must have felt about your
firstborn, choicelessly accepting the responsibility. It was
not quite love, was it? Ambivalence? And you had three
more! I can remember holding a grudge that you couldn't
love me absolutely and exclusively. Now, with my own
ambivalence, I understand how you did love.

As a daughter of a daughter of a daughter, I've taken to
sitting on my porch in the evenings. Comfortably invisible,
I listen to lawn mowers and watch hang gliders push off the
mountain. Alison dozes in her mechanical swing. (We've

nicknamed the swing "grandma"!) A girl friend called,
wanted me to march in a pro-choice rally tonight. Can't go,
I have a week's worth of dishes to do.

Love,
Mara

Making Ends Meet

In Mara's theology only movie stars and welfare mothers could have babies without fathers. When Mara learned she was going to have a baby she kept punching the clock, typing telexes in the textbook department at the university. As the baby grew, Mara sat farther and farther back from the machine.

Because the baby was restless inside her, Mara had asked the manager to change her job title to Administrative Aide. Then, sheepishly, she asked for a raise, the first in her life, explaining that she was head of a household now. The manager took Mara to lunch, noting the blouse over her household shifted from time to time. Gently, he discouraged Mara from seeking the raise, from feeling any loyalty to the corporation. He suggested she look at her options.

So Mara went to Financial Aid, where she was told that she must apply for welfare before qualifying for education loans. Students she talked to reasoned that social programs were the state's investment in its future. The accountant's daughter did not agree and she began to think of night school, even as the date of her grad school exam approached.

The desk in the lecture hall where Mara took the exam in November swung up from beneath the seat. It was not contoured to the shape of Mara's body, but she hunched over the paper filling in the circles to the best of her ability. At two o'clock, a violent kicking began within. Mara fidgeted over the "analytical" portion of the test, which required her to reduce situations to diagrams of circles within circles within squares The foot kicked squarely at her ribs, again and again. Mara looked at the students to either side, intent on their work, and discreetly pushed back at the foot, which after another two minutes kicked again.

Mara's scores came back high in mathematics, higher than in verbal ability. She had wanted to pursue speech pathology, communication disorders, learn to talk with her hands. But she made ambitious applications, having money orders made from the wad of cash stashed in her sock drawer for the application fees. She was turned down at the school in the midwest, within weekend distance of the Johnsons. She decided to stay put. If an assistantship came through, she would go to school full time, and if not, she'd take a night course a semester. She began to proceed as if the assistantship would come through, as on other certainties she could not see. She pushed to share her current job with another graduate student and the manager's answer was no. He would make arrangements for lighter duty. Mara received permission from the dean of the graduate school to work a second job with the assistantship she had yet to receive.

Which was how Mara came to be rolling nickels and dimes behind the bars of the cashier's window. Each morning, she balanced the tills and carried them into the vault, smiling at the picture of Alison on her desk as she emerged. She cashed checks and listened to the sob stories of rich kids who discreetly asked for loans until their CD's matured. She traded vegetarian recipes with divorcées cashing their welfare checks. She felt very, very rich handling the dirty money each day. Mara studied the bars at the cashier's window for Alison's perspective on the world of merchandise: bright backpacks and sweat shirts, notebooks, pens and books, potato chips and condoms.

But it was Mara's father who told her that the secret of making ends meet was not to maintain a car. She walked the eight blocks between campus and family housing twice a day, undisturbed by the sameness of the cinder-block apartments at the base of Mount Sentinel. Each evening she retrieved Alison not from a sitter, but from an entire family of five. In the beginning, leaving her there had been like leaving her left arm behind. Now, Mara stepped deftly through the clutter of children's vehicles in the tiny yard and stood beside the diaper pail on the porch, knocking. Within, she could hear someone say, "Baby Alison, your mommy's here." Alison would crawl toward the door with excitement. As Mara opened the door, she felt momentarily like a father, welcomed home from work. Alison pulled to an unsteady stand, using the hem of her mother's skirt, and began to climb her, like a tree. Mara stooped, saying "How's my girl?" and lifted her daughter high. While Alison hugged her mother and bounced in her arms and squeezed her mother's neck again, the woman of the house patiently swept flour from the floor. It was flour, she explained, Baby Alison had spilled.

Ammunition

Mara had bought the gun three years ago, thinking it might bring them together again. They could sight it in and target practice. They could spend long afternoons driving cross-country, following herds of antelope. Or they could stand on the horizon together, as she'd seen Mac and his dog do so many evenings at sunset.

She'd piled into the pickup with the boys one evening at sunset and driven some forty miles north of the Milk River, through wasteland that reminded her of a moonscape. There was a rifle ranch, a famous gun wholesaler, out there somewhere. She purchased a Ruger 7 × 57 on Mac's recommendation; it would be lightweight and versatile. Jack gave her the 4 power Bushnell scope. Both promised it would someday be a good investment. Mara spent most of her last $300 on it.

In the field, she'd shot it only once, propping the barrel up against the window frame of an open pickup door. She took aim at a herd of antelope some three to four hundred yards away. Mac peered through a pair of binoculars, when the gun recoiled against Mara's shoulder and knocked her glasses askew.

"No, no, not a doe! The buck, the buck."

Mara, shaken, never said as much, but privately she thought her heartbeat caused the errant shot.

Alison wailed when Mara called to see if Mac would like to buy the rifle from her. Christmas was coming, she explained; she needed the money for gifts. Sure, he said, and hung up before they could agree on a price.

Friday afternoon, just before Mara went to pick Alison up at the sitter's, Mac appeared on her doorstep and grinned. They hadn't seen each other in months. "I'm here for the gun."

"Oh. Sure," Mara answered. "But I was just on my way out. Can you wait five minutes? I'll have to dig it out of the closet."

"Sure," he said again. And Mara disappeared.

But by the time she returned, both Alison's father and the gun were gone. The closet was a jumble of receiving blankets and shoes. On Mara's kitchen table lay a $100 bill and a note, "This is all I can afford this month."

She waited another thirty days and called him at the shop. "Can you make another installment on the gun today?"

"You bet."

"Good. Wait there. I'll be by around four."

Mara walked from the bus stop, a good half mile, carrying a case of formula in her hands. She'd left her mittens on the bus. Her skin shrank a bright callous pink against her knuckles, translucent in the November air. She had no watch. She guessed by the color of the sky it must be four thirty or so. A bell tinkled behind her as she entered Lane's shop.

She took a deep breath of warm air and asked for Mac.

"Not here," Lane replied too helpfully.

"Did he leave anything for me?"

Lane played dumb.

Mara asked to use the phone. She explained to the sitter just where she was, that she was on foot and more than likely, she'd be late. "Reassure Alison, I'm coming." In the background, Mara heard a number of indistinguishable cries.

She rubbed her hands together and hoisted the unwieldy box of formula to her hip. "Tell him I stopped by."

As she turned to go, Lane lifted a brand-new $100 bill from his wallet and waved it at her.

Mara set the box down and held out her hand.

For two months then, she thought about the gun as an investment. She figured it must be worth more three years after she bought it. Just before Alison's birthday, Mara decided to collect the third installment. She worried about it for a week, then one Saturday afternoon she bundled Alison up.

It took Mara an hour to cross town on foot. And with each frozen breath, she reviewed the past year. She could remember those first tenuous weeks of Alison's life. All the nights she'd guarded her daughter's breath. The sound of Mara's heartbeat amplified and interfered. Time after time, she jumped from her bed to put her palm against the baby's belly. The only tragedy Mara had been able to imagine was a crib death.

They'd made it, nearly to the age when Mara could cease to worry about such things. They'd made it, Alison strapped to Mara's back. She was going to see her daddy for the first time.

Mara hadn't called to see if he'd be home. She walked briskly as if that didn't matter, as if this were just a walk. Exercise. Her heart began to pound again. She pictured him in an easy chair, his leg propped up, bluing her rifle. She pictured him holding it up to the light and pleased with his work, slipping a cartridge into the chamber, forgetting for the first time in his life to set the safety. Her knock at the door would surprise him. Her face would cause the rifle to discharge.

Alison dozed with one rosy cheek against Mara's shoulder.

He was home. He invited Mara in. He offered her a drink, coffee? Mara shook her head, explained her purpose, inquired about his knee. She could see for herself, the injured knee filled one leg of his jeans like a log. He hobbled off on crutches to his room. Mara watched him, thinking he couldn't be much of a hunter now. She saw him empty his wallet, hobble back across the room. Matter-of-factly, he counted out $65. "There," he said, "we're even."

The glare she had anticipated in his eyes, the same as Alison's warm brown ones, softened. With a callused knuckle, he stroked the sleepy baby under her chin. Mara backed away. She did not see Alison's eyes open and blink and sparkle. Alison smiled at Mac as she would at any man.

Grandpa

Mara called from Denver after she'd stood in line an hour for a standby number and another hour for hotel accommodations. She and Alison were given one number, #228, and as they inched toward the ticket counter, Mara searched for other travelers bound for Kansas City. "We could rent a car and be there by morning," she told a man in a rumpled three-piece suit. "I'd share the driving."

The man looked at Mara, the smelly spot on her coat where Alison had thrown up in Kalispell, and the child using a flight bag for a pillow at her knees. He smiled. "You're right, we could. But the roads are slick and it's snowing. And the airline wants to make sure we get a good night's sleep."

Mara was incredulous. She could see the man's righteous delight in the hotel room he had coming. The same airline had shipped Mara by bus to Kalispell yesterday when Missoula was so enshrouded with fog no plane could land. While she had waited for the fog to lift, guards at the metal detector had unwrapped all her gifts. The airline had offered the bus ticket to Kalispell and room accommodations there, but the flight to Denver had been an hour late in leaving. She had missed her connection to Kansas City. Another room was not the answer.

Mara asked others, a kid in jeans and ski jacket who thought she was kidding, a pair of elderly sisters who said they didn't drive, even a black man who said, "Cars are expensive." "Let's let the airline foot the bill," Mara replied. She shuffled ahead five feet during these conversations, estimating she had another forty-five minutes to wait. She wondered as she waited about America's pioneer spirit.

She and Alison spent a second night in a motel, calling the Johnsons to say she had no idea when they would arrive. New Year's perhaps. Mara described Stapleton as a refugee camp, her efforts to rent a car.

The call that came at seven, saying "Good morning, Mara," was her mother. "I've spent the night on the telephone. You and Alison have a seat on Continental flight 156 at nine thirty. Can you meet it?"

They dressed and took a cab to the airport, walking past the standby line where an airline official called out "Thirty-seven." The plane rose up through the clouds, obscuring the mountains and winter wheat fields below. Mara and Alison breakfasted on muffins and juice in the glorious sunshine at 30,000 feet. They played patty-cake and as Mara explained pictures in the flight magazine she smiled, imagining her mother on the telephone fast-talking the ticket agents and their computers.

But it was Grandpa who waited at the gate in Kansas City. His eyes flickered behind his reading glasses from mother to daughter to mother and back again. He lifted his granddaughter high into the air, giving her a toss that brought squeals.

"Alison, this is your grandpa." Alison reached for his glasses. "And this is Alison."

They stood at the luggage carousel, awaiting Aunt Grace's battered suitcase. Alison grinned at her mother, the lenses magnifying her wide brown eyes. Mara smiled wanly.

Half blind, Mara's father thought he saw the patient set of Mara's mother's face imposed on his own features as he studied his daughter's face, the wisps of hair, the luggage going round.

"There it is." Mara pointed, shouldering the flight bag full of diapers as the suitcase incredibly came her way.

Mara laid her head against the car seat, using the child's trick of closing her eyes to make the last few miles pass more quickly. It seemed less than two minutes before the Buick pulled into the suburban drive. Mara's mother stood on the porch, impatient as a child to hold her granddaughter. She lifted the baby from Grandpa's arms and disappeared upstairs to change Alison's soaking diaper.

"Brrr," Mara's father shivered aloud behind her.

Funny, Mara thought setting down her bag, I don't feel the cold. She searched the branches of the Christmas tree for ornaments she remembered, the beeswax angel with Mara's teeth marks in the wings, Styrofoam drums, and one surviving glass ball distorting the reflection of her face so that it receded from the nose.

"Mara!" she heard her mother holler. "How do you fasten these newfangled diapers?" She came down the stairs with Alison, one side of the paper diaper gaping. Mara rummaged in her bag for a diaper pin, fastening the loose tape backwards over the hip. "There. That's just fine."

Mara's mother quartered oranges for Alison, who sat at the kitchen table sucking them with one tooth and her gums. Mara sat in the overstuffed orange rocker, so full of eggnog she could not remember why she'd left home. Mara's sister sat in her husband's lap, expecting the second grandchild. One brother sat at the piano playing requests: boogie-woogie, "Stardust," and "White Christmas." Another brother watched football. Mara's father sat in the uneasy chair, pushed over to make room for the tree, putting his new trumpet to his lips. He tooted along to a Pete Fountain Christmas album.

Alison climbed down out of her chair to lie in the sunshine on the carpeting at his black-stockinged feet. She had never heard a musical instrument. This one was very shiny, not the dented, dulled trumpet Mara had been disciplined for sneaking out of its worn velveteen case and sputtering on as a kid, the one Dad played in marching band. Grandpa tooted and made a face at Alison. Alison laughed. Grandpa tooted again and said, "Music." He picked up the melody of the piano, "Red Roses for a Blue Lady," forgetting the granddaughter, the daughter, the rest of the family for the music. Mara studied his closed, straining eyelids.

Alison only had eyes for her reflection, distorted in the trumpet's bell. Alison curled at his feet, listening to the music, until she fell asleep.

"When did Dad get the new trumpet?" Mara asked her mother as they set the table for Christmas dinner.

"Oh, it's been several years ago. About the time you left home. Or was it after Grandpa Johnson passed away?" Mara's mother stood between the dining room and kitchen trying to sort out the past, an effort that showed on her face.

"He's much better than I remember."

"He was always pretty good, though he didn't get the trumpet out much while you kids were growing up."

Mara turned to look at her father, asleep now with the trumpet in his lap. In the tousled gray hair, the dark hairs on the gap of white skin between his socks and trousers, she began to see a boy. She thought of the jazz she had inexplicably liked, traveling through the whitened world to fish with Mac. She thought of her blue shadow on the bluer snow.

"Can you remember when we made the relish?" Mara asked her sister. "How we'd mash those cranberries and oranges into the food grinder and take turns with the handle?"

"I remember the stain on the basement floor, spreading newspapers," her sister replied, looking at Alison help herself to a handful of the relish. Mara pushed the dish back. Alison reached again and Mara gently slapped her daughter's hand. She sighed, realizing the first handful was all over Alison's face, and excused herself to wet a washcloth.

As she worked on Alison's face, Mara heard her father say, "Was it necessary to slap her hand?"

Mara sat stunned, staring at her father's mouth. The teeth behind the lips, behind the music? The flash of gold and the tongue. She focused on the mouth, the mustache pursed now around an after-dinner cigarette, having visions of his absences and broken aquariums and soaking carpet and the forbidden trumpet and tomatoes Mara had smashed. The visions swam before her into the metal edge of a ruler and the fly swatter and Mother's distant look. The mouth laughed now, emitting

a curling cloud of smoke, and she looked for the tongue that
told the tales of water balloons dropped from theater balconies
and whitewashing his sister's back, tales he'd told on himself
at this very table. He laughed again and Mara saw the band
march down his tongue. She studied the parts of his mouth
as if by doing so she could understand this joke.

"Mara, you look like you've seen a ghost."

"Uh? Oh," she answered as Alison took an olive and paused,
waiting for the family's response to her latest misbehavior.
Mara passed the child the entire dish of olives. She had not
known whether to scream or laugh at her father. She began
to pry the olives from Alison's hand, one at a time.

Alison cried.

"Don't cry, Alison. That's house rule #1."

In frustration, Alison tossed the entire dish of olives onto
the celery green carpet.

Mara asked patiently, "Alison, honey, why did you do that?"

Mrs. Johnson eyed her daughter with questioning concern.
Mara looked at her mother, playfully staying her from stooping
to clean up the mess. She laid her hand on her mother's freckled
arm.

"Alison," Mara queried, "you must tell us *why* you did
that."

Alison threw her spoon to the floor and began to cry again,
knowing she had misbehaved.

"Back up your assertion with a reason, child."

Alison wailed. She kicked in her high chair, catching the
tablecloth with the toe of one foot.

"The answer is 'just because,' " Mara went on in her perverse
monologue. And as the dishes began to slide from the table,
Mr. Johnson caught the gravy boat in his hands. He stared at
Mara.

While Mr. Johnson disappeared into the kitchen, Mara smiled at her brothers, sister, brother-in-law, scrambling to retrieve pieces of their table settings. She grabbed her mother's hand, making her sit among the ruins of the meal. Furtively, the family members eyed Mara and Mr. Johnson, as he picked up the high chair, moving it baby and all into the kitchen. Alison, already stunned by the sound of falling china and silver, felt jolted as the chair was set down. She whimpered as her grandpa wrestled with the unfamiliar motions of removing a baby from the chair. Roughly, he washed her messy face.

"Mucus," Alison suggested, looking hopefully at her grandpa. To the family members crowded in the kitchen, rinsing plates and loading the dishwasher, Grandpa patiently explained, "That means music."

"How was I?"

"True to form," Mrs. Johnson replied dryly, eyeing the carpet for stains.

"Devil's advocate or single parent, as you were, by default?"

"Forgive him, Mara. He's not the same man."

"I thought you of all people would understand."

"I do. There's more of the accountant left in you than is left in him."

"How's that?"

"Alison will show you."

"Only if I encourage her misbehavior."

"Is that what you think he did?"

"Instead of guidelines, he asked me why."

"And you're whining about that?"

"I don't whine. It's just I've been hearing echoes of why ever since I've been home."

"You want me to tell you why?" Mara shook her head. "You think you left home so he'd know what it was like to lose a child. You left home because he wanted you to, to make your own choices."

"My own mistakes."

"Listen to him."

Mara heard Alison clapping at trumpet music in the next room. "A doting grandpa."

"No, can't you hear the mistakes? Your father improvises." Mara's mother added, "He's not angry at you."

"Disappointed then."

"Actually, he's pleased." Mrs. Johnson said, rising from the table. "He thinks of you as some sort of"—she searched for a word—"pioneer."

"Why doesn't he say so?"

Mara heard her father add a riff to an album of Christmas carols, the hum of the dishwasher.

"Then he wouldn't be your father."

Mara's mother encouraged her to go out, visit old friends, old haunts. "Relax," she said, "I'll watch Alison for you."

Mara drove past the suburban houses childhood friends had grown up in and left behind, down Blue Ridge to Raytown. She took the freeway to the River Quay and parked in an empty stall at the Farmers' Market, listening for the Missouri River. So sluggish beneath the bridges, the sound evaporated into the city's roar. She circled downtown, taking a half hour to remember the one-ways, past the all-night newsstand she didn't dare enter alone. She passed the Lyric Opera, the stage door that led up to Dennis' office, and down Main, to view the hotel where the the dance floor had given way. At Crown

Center, she sat on cold, concrete steps admiring the tiny white lights in deciduous trees. She passed Milton's and the Red Head, turning right onto Westport, studying the crowd for a familiar face. A car honked behind her, as she realized the faces she looked for were up north. Mara counted police cars outside doughnut shops. She parked in front of the apartment she had shared with Dennis, studying the movement of the new tenants within. She circled through Hyde Park, not knowing which houses her friends were renovating, and headed south again. At the Art Institute, she parked, getting out to wander the darkened campus. The statue of the pregnant woman was gone, replaced by the rusted I-beams of environmental art. Mara detoured through the Plaza, admiring each building outlined in its own color of light. She followed Brush Creek, the wide concrete river with a trickle down the center, past the lit fountains gracing the art museum. Stone horses reared back in the cold water. She drove through the university and picked up the Paseo again. This street was so familiar. She followed slow-moving cars through a tunnel of crystalline trees, swinging left and descending into the suburbs again.

Too early to go home, Mara parked a half mile out at a shopping mall and walked to the building. She window-shopped, dogged by her own reflection, thinking perhaps a movie, a drink. She went into the bar of one restaurant and ducked out again, put off by the overdone decor. She counted shoe stores and walked slowly back to the car. Mara studied the sky for the stars she could connect with a finger up north. Her eyes followed the lights of a plane until it was out of sight.

"I'm back."
Mara's mother sat up in bed.

"Anybody up?" Mara called, coming up the stairs. She sat on the edge of her parents' bed, whispering, "It's awfully quiet. How'd it go?"

"Alison cried herself to sleep."

"But she's never had to do that before," Mara hissed. "How long did she cry?"

"An hour or so. Your father got out his old battered horn and played Taps for her." Mara smiled. "You remember when he played Taps for you?"

Mara nodded. "Vaguely. Guess I'll go to bed. We've got a long day ahead of us tomorrow."

The return flight bypassed Denver for Salt Lake. Passengers jockeyed their assigned seats so that Alison could have the extra seat and her mother could sit beside her. But the Salt Lake flight flew over Missoula's fog, Kalispell's, and landed in Great Falls. Missoula passengers were bussed over the Continental Divide. Mara rode with Alison's head in her lap.

Shelly met their bus. She lifted Alison's deadweight from her mother's arm, leaving Mara to search for their luggage. "How was the trip?" she asked Alison.

Mara answered for her daughter, "She's in love with her grandpa."

Uncle

Alison's face lit up at the still, distinct, familiar pieces of furniture that materialized when Mara turned on the living room light. She crawled the room, touching their familiar things, as Mara shuffled through the mail. Among the bills and newspapers that had collected for Mara in her absence was a small package for Alison and a Christmas card dimly post-marked Ma——a, MT. Alison set to work on the brown wrapping as her mother settled into the loveseat to read, "Best Wishes for the New Year."

Alison struggled with the cellophane tape and Mara helped absentmindedly, recalling her one Christmas there. The tree they'd selected from a hillside in the Little Rockies, studded with candles set in aluminum foil stars and candy canes and crocheted snowflakes. Alice's fear that the candlelit tree in the basement would set her boardinghouse on fire. Their awe at the moon of light the tree created on the ceiling of the basement apartment. The filet knife Alice had given Mara Christmas morning.

Alison gave up the struggle, coming to a bright red paper covered with snowmen. Mara skimmed paragraphs of weather and car troubles and health problems. She slowed, forcing herself to read the mimeographed paragraph about Mac's brother at the same rate she would read about the sisters, and Mac. Joe was still teaching school. Jennifer was expecting her first child in January. Mara smiled, remembering Jennifer as the sister who made caramels and rosettes and set the table for Christmas brunch just right. Ambrosia for breakfast and then games of Monopoly and cards at the same table, with gifts and wrappings cluttering the living room. Jody, the youngest sister, who was in secretarial school now in Calgary, hollered at Mac, "You cheat, you cheat."

Mac quit. The bubbles in the Canadian Club and soda went slowly flat in the drink Jody made to keep her brother home. Mac and Mara had gone downtown in weather 20 degrees below zero to drink hot buttered rums. Mara had been surprised at the number of people in the bar on Christmas Day. Mac had gone up and down the bar slapping displaced persons on the back. "Spreading cheer," he said.

Mara had sat patiently, watching the clock, thinking she ought to call Kansas City. But more people came, dancers took to the floor, drinks lined up before her.

She had tugged on Mac's sleeve, suggesting they go home. Mac had laughed at the joke his friend on the next barstool was telling and ignored her. She tried to stand and the room swayed. She steadied herself, grabbing at Mac's shirt. "Mac, I think I'm getting drunk."

"Go for a walk, that'll sober you up." His friend had laughed with Mac at the suggestion. The temperature. Mara missed the humor and made for the door without her coat. The air jolted her and she took deep breaths, studying the still mannequins in caps and mittens in the Penney's window, the decorative angel hair beneath the drugstore's display of gifts. Mara walked around the block, her footprints straightening as she breathed.

Taking her seat again beside Mac, she had said, "It worked." Mara started in on another rum, watching nine approach. "Mac," she said to no one in particular, "do you know any of these people?" "Mac, my parents may be trying to call. We better go home." And finally, "Mac, I'm sick." Mara had slumped against him.

"Go take another walk."

That time Mara had taken her down jacket, but she lacked the coordination to zip it closed. She walked the opposite direction around the block. The temperature had dropped, somewhere further below zero. She could tell by the way her fingers ached, her forehead froze. She walked twice around the block, hoping Mac would come after her. And then she had stumbled down an alley, slipping on the ice.

Mara had stood, the hairs in her nose frozen stiff. Her nose felt full of needles. Alarmed, she knew if Mac could see her now he would only think "drunken Indian" and drive on by. She knew she had less than twenty minutes to walk to the boardinghouse and that she mustn't fall or think of lying down to sleep. She knew she must walk down the middle of the street, so if she fell they'd find her soon.

She had put her palm to her forehead, trying to warm her headache away, then put her hands between her legs. She pulled her coat up around her ears and pulled it down, putting her hands in her pockets. She had moaned in the streets, falling and sobbing and standing. "Look at me, look at me," thinking unclearly, "I'm a native at last." And then laughing in the intersection, studying the streets that spread in three directions around her, "Which way is home?"

Mara had braced herself, walking two blocks east and one block south. Mac's dog had raced out to meet her, with Mara's gift to Mac in its mouth. Mara fought the dog for the Pendleton shirt, not even unpinned from its cardboard. As the collar ripped away, Mara sat in the snow crying, "Momma, Momma."

Alice had stuck her head out the door, demanding, "Who's there?"

"Momma," Mara had moaned, as Alice turned on the porch light. She shuffled down the steps, into the snow, in pink scuffs.

"Mara? Come on, child, stand up."

Mara stood and forced her legs to step down the basement stairs. Alice had guided her to bed and removed the coat. She had held Mara's hands between her own, chafing them. She stroked Mara's features with a warm washcloth. She held Mara's head against her breast, ignoring the girl's drunken explanations, Mac this, Mac that. Alice had rocked Mara until her sobs subsided, saying, "Sleep now, sleep now." Mara, warmed by a wonderful shame, closed her eyes.

"Mac has gone to work in the mines. Don't know what he does, but the confidentiality suits him." Alice's mimeographed letter marveled that Mac had stuck with the same job for over a year.

A chill passed through Mara as she read a line scribbled at the bottom of the page: "You should probably know that Tuff passed away in July. Mac wouldn't harvest this year—said

Alison had more original blood in her than Mary Lou. But the gleanings, Mara, are better without him. Hope you won't mind my sending along a little something for Alison this Christmas."

Mara studied the little body curled in sleep around the gift she couldn't open. Mara untied the flattened ribbon, the paper. She studied the knit cap and mittens. She put Alison to bed still in her traveling clothes, unable to comprehend this news, Mac's gift.

Scavengers

Mara walked. She had been walking since Alison was a colicky baby. In the evenings after work, she bundled her baby in a light flannel blanket, descended a flight of stairs, and turned left, waiting at the corner for traffic to pass. They crossed the street and headed west on South Avenue, walking. The baby was consoled by the motion of her mother's body, the hum of traffic, an occasional word, a name for a thing.

A woman on her way home from the grocery stopped, telling Mara how much better it was that Mara walked, muttering about these mothers on bicycles with kids strapped into seats and their heads flopping around like Raggedy Anns. "You support her head." Mara nodded as the woman peeked under the blanket, meeting Alison's eyes.

Mara walked for blocks, some nights around and around the same block, other nights up a residential street and down an alley. Drivers felt that they'd come to know the pair, and honked and waved. They walked. And as the sun set, Mara uncovered Alison's face and they walked. Leaves fluttering overhead fascinated the baby. The spaces between leaves. The shift of light on her face. They walked and the streetlight came on, magically it seemed to Mara, though Alison believed the lights responded to her gaze. They walked and Mara began shyly to sing her strange repertoire of songs, the ABC's and "Amazing Grace" and "Bicycle Built for Two." She sang low, shy of being heard by homeowners watering their lawns. And her voice cracked. Alison studied the spaces between her mother's words. And closed her eyes and listened for the vibration within her mother's chest. She began to sleep, and Mara pivoted and retraced the mile or two home.

At twelve pounds, Alison outgrew her mother's arms, and riding in a backpack, she waved at the neighbors who expected this spectral mother and child every evening, without knowing their names. She picked leaves from trees overhead as Mara walked. She munched crackers from the endless supply in her mother's pocket and fell asleep, drooling in her mother's hair.

At thirty pounds, Mara's back began to ache. She and Alison rode downtown on the bus and bought a wagon. Alison rolled home behind Mara, who bent to lift it down and up and over curbs. She rode, feeling the difference in texture between sidewalk and street, dirt and grass, and ice and snow. From time to time, the wagon tipped and Alison cried and helped Mara gather their spilled groceries. Or Alison raided the groceries, taking bites out of hot dogs or tomatoes, or devouring whole grapes. Alison sat backwards in the wagon. Mara pulled and Alison watched where they'd been. She sat at the far end, dangling her legs and dragging her scuffed shoes.

Mara, who once was made dizzy by the movement of clouds in the sky or the changing of seasons, liked this pace, but she was impatient when Alison began to walk. Alison stumbled and stood. She stooped to study an insect mashed on the sidewalk. She examined pine needles and helicopter seeds, holding them up for Mara to "see." She loitered over "pitty rocks" and Mara had to go back to retrieve her. Or she ran to catch up, handing her mother a windfallen apple.

Mara sat in the apartment watching Alison's meanderings through the picture window. Alison picked a dandelion, a sprig of timothy, and brought them to Mara, saying "Guess." And Mara said, "Umbrella?" Alison shook her head. "Shell?" Again, Alison shook her head. "Penny?" "No," Alison cried, delighted with her mother's ignorance. She held out her hand to show Mara a sweaty blue-gray feather.

Alison wandered up the mountain and brought home the first buttercup, a tick, and a blade of sharp grass she said was a sword. She brought home a cracker and pulled Mara out of the house to show her where she got it, so Mara made a friend. She brought home a newspaper, so Mara made an enemy. She came home with one bare foot. Mara asked, "Where's your shoe?" and Alison shrugged. She brought home a stalk of wild asparagus, so Mara began to walk again.

They walked farther and farther from home, studying pools of minnows in Rattlesnake Creek, corn in the droppings of dogs, the tread of bicycles in the dust, a hoofprint in the snow, a steak bone, a rusted railroad spike Alison couldn't lift. From the top of Mount Sentinel, they watched a train crawl through the valley like a worm. Mara became so absorbed in the minutiae of Alison's world, she was no longer paralyzed by the grandeur of mountains, the crowded larch, cozy pink houses, plaid shirts, rifle racks, and animals with trees sprouting from their heads.

Alison's Father

In Mara's circle of acquaintances, there was a divorced sawyer friend of Mac's who, after trying to talk some sense into Mara, unearthed his son's warped crib from a shed. He gave it to a Cat skidder for refinishing. The skidder believed that before he could ask a woman for a date he must have bought and paid for every woodworking tool and household appliance and for a fancy car. Yet he spent hours during Mara's pregnancy sitting with her at the kitchen table. There were anonymous hunters who left packages of frozen meat on Mara's doorstep. There was a bachelor of sixty-five, a co-worker of Mara's, who drove her to a lumberyard for bricks and boards, and wanted only for her to drink a beer with him in a public place.

She met a writer of pulp westerns who told Mara sincerely "you are lovely" before she confided the reason for her radiance. Over omelets, he detailed the plot of his next book. A smoke jumper with a cast on one leg took Mara to hear mandolin jazz. And a poet, blind in one eye since his days as a premie in an oxygen tent, hiked with Mara even as her pelvis spread. A fisherman wanted Mara to sit on the riverbank in silence.

There were men out of her past. One, a gunsmith, offered to pay medical expenses. Mara explained that she would rather owe money to corporations than her friends. Alan, a welder who grew melons, brought Mara fresh produce. Jim called from Minneapolis, emboldened by cocaine, and asked Mara to marry him. Dennis sent Alison a panda bear puppet that frightened her as it came to life on Mara's hand. A labor organizer who read old newspapers like novels supplied Mara with caps and mittens from the university's lost and found. A divorced philosophy major writing a thesis on Hamlet plied Mara with coffee. A doctoral candidate in psychology arranged for a sitter and cooked Mara a candlelit meal. Mara even knew a sad Marxist with a vasectomy. And there were women who told Mara their sad stories and sat back waiting for her sympathy.

Peter, a physician who never practiced because he did not like people, taught Alison to fly and told Mara that breast-feeding *was* a reliable form of birth control. A hospital administrator raising four children alone carried Mara's wet laundry. An ex-cop who frequented the taxidermy studio sent a check for $50. A textbook salesman sent Alison a copy of *Mother Goose*. Bill, a retired rancher who could predict calving within twenty-four hours by the elasticity of the heifer's pelvis, brought Alison a hypoallergenic teddy bear and urged Mara into therapy. Lee, the conscientious objector, confided to Mara, "Most men are afraid of you." Gregg got down on all fours, crawling the apartment with Alison on his back.

Mara had thought most men felt a misplaced pity for mother and child. She didn't mean to frighten them. In fact, she was generous, offering them what they wanted, explaining ahead of time her house rule. She found they were very choosy after all, getting up and putting on their clothes. All except one.

First Kiss

On weekends, Mara showed Alison what to do with flour on
the floor. Together, they kneaded the dough until it began to
take on life and resist their hands. They let it rise and punched
it down again, folding laundry and washing dishes as they
waited. Alison pulled a chair to the rinse side of the divided
sink, where she poured and mixed water.

One Saturday, there was a knock at the door. Mara answered,
drying suds from her hands. It was a man who explained he'd
seen Mara's ad for a Monday night sitter on the laundry room
wall. The man explained he would be willing to do it for free
as part of a child development course he was taking. Mara
invited him in, asked him to tell her about himself. He hes-
itated, apologizing for the way he smelled. "All my clean
clothes are in the wash." Mara sniffed, pine pitch and manure.

Alison grinned and waved with excitement, sitting in the
rinse water. She recognized the man. He was her mother's
height, with so many muscles even she recognized the vul-

nerability inside. He had a salt and pepper beard with an unruly auburn patch. His mouth chuckled at her as the water overflowed the sink onto the floor. She recognized this man because he had his glasses on. He was the one she'd seen sitting in the tree house, a pair of binoculars dangling from his neck, with a finger to his lips. She'd found him on the walk when her mother had been so impatient. Mara had stood on the sidewalk thirty feet ahead, hollering "What are you staring at? Hurry up!" as Alison looked up into the tree.

He began to baby-sit on Monday nights. He sat right down on the floor and helped Alison build structures out of alphabet blocks. Alison knocked them down, coyly trying to make him laugh. But he was very patient. They started over again and again. Alison built highways and bridges, stairs and windows. The baby-sitter required her to pick up her toys.

Then he would put her jammies on. Together they rummaged through the cupboards looking for a bedtime snack. He offered Alison a choice, graham crackers or raisins. She slammed his finger in the cupboard door. She wanted a sweet pickle and they were in the fridge. The baby-sitter located Alison's blankie, out in the yard, and the teddy bear that sucked its thumb. He tucked Alison in and closed the bedroom door, watching television until Mara came home.

Alison heard them asking one another what they'd learned tonight. She climbed out of her crib and listened at the door to the strange sound of her mother's laughter. The baby-sitter wasn't laughing. He held up the swollen tip of his finger, saying Mommy's "benign 'difference" had gone far enough. He said Alison was spoiled and needed some "displine."

Mara related what had happened the day they'd posted the baby-sitting ad. Alison's hand had caught in the pneumatic door. Mara had felt the pain of it in her own belly. "Alison isn't being mean. She wants to know if your hand hurts too."

Alison fingered her navel. Soon, she heard the door close and climbed back into bed.

The next Monday night, the baby-sitter flexed his pecs to make Alison laugh. He played imaginary piano and tap-danced in his boots. Alison served him a tea party, salads of lettuce, sweet pickles, and chocolate syrup. The baby-sitter kissed Alison good night and tucked her into bed.

In the dark, Alison wrote on the wall with crayon. She retrieved the sitter to show him her handiwork. The baby-sitter smiled. "That's nice. Very nice." He put Alison back to bed, the crayons on top of the refrigerator.

She heard him tell her mommy and covered her ears. The popcorn popper began to pop. Alison could smell it, and she uncovered her ears. She heard the baby-sitter confide, "I've heard toothpaste will take crayon off walls."

"The End," Mara heard the baby-sitter read.

"You're a deadly reader," she said as she let herself in a week later. She nodded at Alison who had fallen asleep on the baby-sitter's bicep.

The baby-sitter smiled.

"What were you reading? Let me guess—*Snow White?*"

The baby-sitter held up a copy of *Beauty and the Beast.*

"Wrong story," Mara said, as the weight of her sleepy child molded itself to her side. "Hopeless romantic."

"And you're not?" the baby-sitter said to Mara's back.

Mara laid Alison in bed, admiring the deliberateness of her sleep, the sweat creating curls along her hairline.

"How can I be?" Mara answered minutes later, as the sitter stood in the doorway.

"What?"

"A romantic," Mara answered, peeved he'd forgotten.

He ventured, "Next Monday night?"

Mara nodded, doorknob in hand, impatient for him to leave. For a moment, she was afraid he was going to kiss her when Alison began to whimper in the blinding bathroom light.

"I'm home," Mara sang. "Alison! Michael? I'm home."

Her voice echoed in the dim apartment. She checked the kitchen table for a note, noting only that the dishes in the drainer were clean and dripped dry. She wandered their rooms, looking at Alison's things, her own. Nervously, she opened and closed a closet door. Mara fondled items on her desk, picked up a stray toy. She collapsed on her sofa, listening, waiting for the distinct sound of Michael's truck to pull up outside.

She felt the vibration of the truck travel through the ground, up into the apartment, the furniture, into her bones. Mara went out to meet them, too calmly asking "What'd you two do tonight?" Alison licked contentedly at a chocolate cone.

"Sorry we're late," Michael said, coming around the truck cavalierly to open Alison's door. "Here, these are for you."

He handed Mara a grocery sack her arms found unexpectedly light. "We went for a drive," he explained, struggling with Alison's seat belt. Mara peered into the sack, a profusion of pale pink petals, leaves, thorns. The faint fragrance of wild roses, hundreds of them.

"Who," Mara asked warily, "picked these?" Alison straddled Michael's hip at eye level. Steadily, Mara looked into their faces.

"Me!" Alison volunteered.

"We," Michael corrected her.

When Mara returned the following Monday, she was locked out of her apartment. Through the tiny window in the door, she saw Alison sitting up with her blanket, studying the block house she'd built, and the baby-sitter passed out on the couch. Mara pounded on the door and Alison started. Mara's daughter padded across the room and wrestled with the knob. Mara pounded on the door and Alison cried that she could not unlock it. Mara pounded on the door and the baby-sitter roused, sat, and slowly put his glasses on. Mara pounded furiously, and the baby-sitter let her in.

"You're supposed to be watching . . ." she said to the baby-sitter. He listened to Mara's angry tirade.

"Did you see what we built?"

But Mara whisked Alison off to her room, tossing the blanket into the crib after the child and brusquely shutting the door. Alison heard excited murmurs beyond her bedroom door, voices rising "Do you have any idea" and falling "to be both" and rising "supportive and firm?"

Alison climbed out of the crib, dragging her blanket. She pried at her bedroom door and walked sleepily into the bright living room light. She blinked and softly whined, "Mommy?"

"I have half a mind to end this arrangement."

"Mommy, my tummy hurts."

"Do you think you can stay awake another Monday night?"

"Mommy, see what we made?"

"Don't you have anything to say for yourself?"

Mara and Michael sat facing one another at the kitchen table. Alison stood between them. Her blanket slipped from her arms. The baby-sitter bent to pick the blanket up, as Mara continued, "I can't miss the—" Alison covered her mother's moving lips with her right hand. The baby-sitter sat up. He cleared his throat, as Alison put her left hand to his lips.

Alison stood with her short arms extended, silencing and connecting their mouths, until her mother looked at the block house.

A NOTE ON THE TYPE

The text of this book was set in a digitized version of Garamond No. 3, a modern rendering of the type first cut by Claude Garamond (c. 1480–1561). Garamond was a pupil of Geoffroy Tory and is believed to have based his letters on the Venetian models, although he introduced a number of important differences, and it is to him we owe the letter that we know as "old style." He gave to his letters a certain elegance and a feeling of movement that won for their creator an immediate reputation and the patronage of Francis I of France.

Composed by PennSet, Inc., Bloomsburg, Pennsylvania

Printed and bound by Fairfield Graphics,
Fairfield, Pennsylvania

Typography and binding design by Julie Rowse-Duquet